D0885281

To Aire Is Divine

Further Tips
Tricks and Tales
About Airedale Terriers

Stories by the members of Airedale-L
Sherry Rind, editor

Contents 🐾

Introduction: The Airedale's Place 🐾

Like Houses Full of Laughter, the previous book by the members of Internet discussion group Airedale-L, this book contains plenty of "guess what my Airedale did today" stories. In addition, To Aire is Divine includes special chapters on puppies and training, along with helpful real-life tips throughout its pages. It is not by any means a dog care or training book. Rather, it offers solutions to questions that come up in everyday life with Airedales, questions you may not find in your usual dog care book because the Airedale (ADT) is not your usual dog.

People living with Airedales agree that obedience training for the dogs is as important as basic table manner training for human children and often more rewarding because Airedales think training is fun. They also like to eat all their vegetables. Obedience training serves the double purpose of making the dog a well-mannered family member and establishing the humans as pack leaders. This is important if you want to be able to open your own refrigerator or climb into your own bed without having to get the dog's permission. An overly assertive dog is truly not funny. Being unable to move or even wake the sleeping Airedale sprawled on your side of the bed is entirely different. For some reason, even the exhausted ADT owner who has worked a long day while his dog played and slept seems to find this amusing.

Unlike the dog who growls if you approach when it is eating or lying on your bed, the sleeping Airedale is not disturbing the proper pack order. He is simply throwing himself fully into the task of the moment, as ADTs tend to do. This distinction between overly-dominant dog and fully-engaged dog becomes important when the Airedale's place as family member, not just family dog, is understood.

When people refer to ADTs as "furkids," they are not anthropomorphizing dogs unduly, nor are they being cute. They are pointing out that the ADT as family member has his own place, different from that of human (upright) child, significant other, friend, or in-law. It is very difficult to define what that place is, however, since the place is everywhere. People who do not allow their spouse of twenty-five years to accompany them into the water-closet allow in the Airedale because the dog expects to be there and is not self-conscious. The Airedale sits on the couch and the person sits on the floor because the dog looks so cute with her head on the arm rest that no one wants to disturb her. People, such as myself, who hate cooking the family dinner happily slave in the kitchen to prepare special treats for the dogs who would be just as happy with a plain piece of cheese as the special doggie birthday cake.

When you think about it, the Airedale does nothing to deserve this royal treatment but be himself. She slurps up water, dribbling a quart on the floor, then rubs her dripping beard on your leg in the notorious WETBEARDKISS. He greets friends, strangers, and dignitaries with a BIGNOSEPOKE to the crotch-no mere sniff this but a high impact greeting. She makes you smile by doing the HAPPYDANCE with all four feet prancing and dancing in a dozen directions, and then she tucks in tail and hind end for a scamper around the house in the famous TUCKBUTTRUN. You may go to a religious service and plan very seriously during the sermon on how to be a better person. How much time do you suppose your dog spends reflecting on how to be a better Airedale? You are probably relieved that he does not.

Yet, not one of the Airedales you will meet in this book would ever be called "only a dog" because there is no "only" about Airedales. Quite the opposite. Author Gertrude Stein once dismissed a certain American city by saying, "*There* is no there there." She might have described Airedales as having an abundance of there-in your face, underfoot, on your lap, under your arm, and in your pockets.

Soon your ADT becomes a reference point. Everywhere you go, you start to watch for signs of Airedale. If you see one, you find yourself running after him and his person to start a conversation with a complete stranger, even if you are normally shy. You start walking around with an Airedale-like grin on your face. When you shop, you buy every Airedale-related thing you can find; more often, you buy two of each. If you travel without your dogs, you soon talk about needing an Airedale "fix."

As homo sapiens you have been attuned since birth to recognize the human face as a member of your species, yet you now start reacting in a similar manner to the Airedale face. You start having long discussions with your dogs and giving clear, one-word commands to your family and business associates. You consistently misspell "air" as "aire."

You also acquire a bounce in your step, a smile when you wake on even the grumpiest days-because the dog is happy-an eagerness to play with new toys, an improved sense of fun and humor, a higher activity level, and increased tenacity. If you succeeded in training your Airedale even minimally, you will feel a competence that pervades your entire being. Most important, when living with an Airedale and giving it the kind of love it gives you, you may find you have acquired a more generous and loving heart. That is where the Airedale will remain a vivid presence long after he has left this earth.

Unfortunately, some people appear to be immune to ADT charm. In these cases, Airedale Rescue comes in to re-home the unwanted, the mistreated, or those who have lost their families due to unfortunate circumstances. Houses Full of Laughter raised over $6,000 for Airedale Rescue in direct contributions to the Rescue branch of the Airedale Terrier Club of America Inc., (www.airedale.org) and money raised by Rescue groups who purchased copies at cost for resale. The book was distributed in the United States, Canada, Australia, parts of Europe, and a few copies found their way to Singapore and Russia. In addition, we held back seed money to print this book, money originally donated by the Clarkes of Care-A-Lot Pet Supply Warehouse (800-343-7680/ www.carealotpets.com).

Profits from the sale of this book, too, will be donated to Airedale Rescue, which locates, fosters, trains, grooms, and provides medical care for Airedales in need of new homes. They carefully screen both dogs and applicants to find the best permanent, loving home. In the Rescue chapter of this book, you will read accounts by listmembers of some of the ADTs they have fostered or adopted and how, in time, the dogs came to feel safe and secure enough to blossom into being "just an Airedale" in all their ever-surprising ways.

Sherry Rind, Editor July, 1999

CHAPTER ONE
The Interior Airedale

THIS CHAPTER REFERS to the Airedale as interior decorator and indoor animal, with a brief foray into Airedale fashion sense. When the ADT is in the house, you know about it. If you do not know about it, then you had better go check to see what the dog is doing. Experienced ADT owners should probably be watched as well, because they have distinct ideas about where the dog belongs in the house-on the furniture, at the hot tub, in the bathroom.

I'm so happy that I just have to tell someone (or everyone, as the case may be). Beau just got on the couch-all four feet for the first time since we got him last spring. My poor darling had somehow got it into his head that he wasn't allowed up there or on the bed either. He saw the girls up on the couch and bed all the time but for some reason just didn't think he belonged. Today he came running when I whistled for him and sort of launched himself. I think he was more surprised than I was. I just scratched his ears and told him what a wonderful baby he was. He didn't stay too long and wouldn't put his head down but it is a step. I know I should be grateful that I have one less 'dale fighting for the couch but I'm not. I like to cuddle with my babies. Now, if I could just get that tail of his wagging like Rosie's does, I'd be all set.

D'Arlene-Anne Kapenga

We spent Christmas at Belding-a small town outside of Grand Rapids, Michigan, where Becky grew up-visiting her parents, brother and his wife, and her parents' Irish Terriorist who will be 1 year old in a few months.

At our house the pups are permitted on the furniture; but in Belding at Becky's parents' home, they are not allowed on the couch, although Meaghan is allowed in grandpapas' recliner! So it is the middle of the night after Christmas Day and I rouse myself out of the torture rack (better known as the guest hideabed) to respond to nature's call. Entering the hall, I look to the living room and see the following: Meaghan is on the floor looking admiringly at Bilbo who is smiling back at her from his sprawled out position ON THE COUCH! and Frodo (Mister Obedient) is sprawled out on Meaghan's dog bed. A few hours later when I hear Becky's parents getting up I also hear Bilbo as he crawls off the couch to lie on the floor when her parents emerge from their room!

Are these dogs smart or what!

Skip Barcy

We took Tavish to visit a friend at Xmas one year. While our friend went out to the kitchen, Tavish casually walked over to the tree and .... yup.

Kate Middleton

Our ADT George (RIP 1990) loved going to the kennel when we traveled. However, soon as he was back at home-into the living room and a quick squat. The first time I was so shocked I couldn't move. After the next trip, I walked him outdoors for about 30 minutes (no go)-into the house and he pooped before I could stop him. Third time, followed him into the living room, inserted wad of newspaper under his rear thinking to at least protect the carpets. He was soooo upset by this and demanded to be let out. Next trip he started his usual game, I started flapping my arms and yelling "NO" so he scooted to the next carpeted area with me flapping and yelling right behind him. This went on for 5 minutes until he tired of the game and willingly went out doors. Dogs!

Ellana Livermore

Last evening we were sitting in the living room and Bannon was lying in her usual place near the doorway into the den, chewing on whatever it was she had found-usually one of her chewy hooves. Suddenly she yelped once, leapt to her feet, and just stared straight down at the floor-no cocking the head, no pawing, no playful stance, just staring. Finally she began to walk around the "spot" as an animal would stalk a poised snake.

We thought it must be a spider, cricket, etc.; however, once she began to walk, we could see that the "snake" was actually a live electrical cord that had been hidden/buried in a crack running along the doorway! After very seriously walking around the shocking toy a few times, she plopped down to study it some more. The cord was crooked up into the air in an upside down "U" shape, about 10" high, and Bannon just lay on the floor eye-level with it, staring, staring, staring. Finally she relaxed enough to begin cocking her head and getting brave again. By this time my husband had examined the cord, realized that it had been bitten well through, and we knew that she had been shocked. We were also thankful that, considering the possibility of saliva in her mouth, she wasn't seriously injured! But does an Airedale care? Does she walk away and find another interest? Of course not!! She decides that here is something that will fight back and is something to be conquered! She finally began to paw at the cord, but still with a very serious stare. We were laughing so hard at her unusual way of dealing with this, that we were distracting her, but she was determined. My husband finally wrapped the cut with electrical tape and took care of the cord so that it is no longer a danger.

Gwen Bagget

Just when we thought we had Cody (RIP now) housebroken, I went my merry way to work leaving him sequestered in his area of the house, the newly renovated family room. He sat at the baby gate and watched me leave, big brown, dewy eyes pleading for me to stay and play just a little while longer.

I came home at lunchtime, not five miles and precisely four

hours later. There was Cody waiting patiently at the gate, waiting for me to tell him what a good boy he had been. Tail wagging. Happy paws dancing. I unlocked the gate. He Happy Danced through the house. I opened the back sliding doors and out he went. I turned around. Behind me was a strange blue popcorn. I could not identify it. It was positively everywhere-on the sofa, loveseat, recliner, bookshelves, TV, windowsills, even! I walked closer. I bent down. I picked up a few pieces. FOAM. Eee- gads! What had he been into? My mind raced. I frantically looked about. Living room, kitchen, laundry room, bedrooms, bathrooms. All were intact. I rubbed the pieces around in my hand as I pondered their origin. CARPET PAD. The wall to wall was in place. I finally recognized the color. Oriental rug padding. Family room. The rug was in place! In place and in perfect shape! I pulled it back. Yup. He had pulled the rug back, "played with" the padding, let the rug drop back into place and had a grand old time playing with, shredding and destroying the carpet pad.

Four out of 5 of us laughed ourselves silly. Two out of 5 of us could not stifle our giggles when The Husband came home. The Husband had NO clue because, just as I'd found it, he saw a room intact (I had cleaned up the popcorn). When I told him what had happened he was not amused (well, not nearly as much as Cody and I were). Ah, the things they leave us with, eh?

Judie Burcham

We recently installed a hot tub in our backyard and on these cold, fall evenings it's been great to relax in the hot, bubbling tub. I watch the stars, enjoy the peaceful, quiet rain falling while I'm warm and safe in the hot tub. Then I feel hot Airedale breath sniff-sniffing in my ear. I reach back and touch, slimy whiskers. Beau is fascinated with the hot tub. He stands right at the edge of the tub wearing a concerned expression on his face.

Judy Dwiggins

I'm goofing off for a few minutes from doing housework while the husband and grandson are out fishing. Also watching 2001 for the umpteen millionth time. Cats inside wanting out and vice versa. Need to vacuum the couches but dogs are sleeping on them with one eye open, saying, "I don't want to move." One of these days am going to decide if it's easier to put a sheet on the couch and take it off when people come over or put it on the couch when people come over. Especially since it's the dog's couch. We use the chairs. Or tell the people to have a seat and ask "dog hair, what dog hair?" That's along with "Oh, you saw the dog with his tongue on the food? That's all right, it won't hurt him." Not that I don't prefer my food non-dog tested; it's just that they're sneaky , devious, and I had my back turned while it was just lying there so they had to make sure it was safe. I also have some swampland and a couple of bridges for sale.

Bev Davidson

Now that I have inherited (MOOCHED is more like it) a queensize bed from my mother, Rita has been gently climbing up and stretching out alongside me to sleep. Last night, she stole in sometime past the hour that the sandman visited, and I neither felt nor heard her snuggle in next to me. About three in the morning, I heard her softly growl. Ellie had roused, and was standing by the bed, reaching and snuffling, looking for me. The Lovely Rita had no taste for any kind of coup, and put Ellie in her place by cranking up the growl and standing, then looming over Ellie to cower her with the intense Royal Rita Stare. Ellie silently slunk out of the room, head down, tail down, but eyes sparkling. SHE had a plan. I, having been roused by this power play, stretched out and hung my hand and both feet off the sides of the bed. By and by, I felt the touch of a cold tentative nose on my fingers, then, a small, sweet puppykiss.

I raised myself up, and in the glow of the screen saver in the next room I saw the form of Ellie, low to the ground and quite proud of herself. She had slunk in on her belly, avoiding Rita's vigilance, until she, too, was able to make first contact with the Mother Ship, in the dark of summer's night.

Gena Welch

Last time I bought a mattress for the guest room, I told the clerk it couldn't be too high, because it was for Tavish-he couldn't jump high when he got older because of his hip dysplasia. I thought the clerk was going to pass out. After he asked, "You're getting it for who?" five times, he was nearly screaming about me letting a dog on one of these bee-oo-tiful mattresses. Poor thing.

Kate Middleton

Just as I was thinking that we were lucky after the discussions about ADTs and Xmas trees, Lady Darwin, (17 months) has attacked ornaments on our tree on 2 consecutive days. The Teddy Principle definitely applies. The tree had been up for 3 weeks before she did any mischief. On both occasions, everyone was upstairs and she was alone in the living room. Both the ornaments that she destroyed had a great deal of red colour on them, resulting in several pink areas on my beige carpet. I was able to get a lot of the colour out but we will have to do a more thorough carpet clean after the tree comes down. To get her mind off the tree and its treasures, I gave her an early Christmas present-a Rhino bone. She absolutely loves it-takes it everywhere with her. What a way to get a new toy!

Mary Henderson

If you fold an old mattress pad (preferably full or queen) inside a king-sized pillowcase, this fits perfectly into 400 hard plastic crate. Toby can get rather naughty with linens (she tries to eat towels and she's still humping our pillow shams), but she has been a perfect lady with this crate mat. Inexpensive, too.

Jessica Rabin

Howard started humping his blanket when he was about five months old-we called it the Friday night special. Anyway, we got him fixed. When he came home, he picked up his blanket and looked confused, as if he knew he wanted to do something, but he couldn't remember what. Hooray, I thought.

I was wrong. Gradually, he remembered how, and is now back to humping, generally on Friday nights. Don't ask me why on Friday nights, except maybe he is more bored because we are so exhausted that we just sit on the couch and stare at the TV.

Betsy Earls

I put in an aquarium this past week and a friend who is moving brought over her tank full of fish and released them last night in my tank. Well, I thought my kitties, all three of them, would be excited as could be to have fish. The cats could not care less about these new additions, but Charlie my one year old ADT is already plotting ways to get them critters out of that tank. We have ADT tongue sliding, paw scraping, and of course that famous ADT nose bumping taking place across the glass of the aquarium. It is too funny to watch. That tongue sliding across 30" of glass is totally ADT watermania. I think Charlie is goin' fishin'.

My fish tank is part of my entertainment center. I built a piece of furniture that would house and hide the TV, serve as a plant display and have the fish tank at ground level. Charlie likes these fish so much that last night he decided to dismantle the entertainment center bite by bite. He removed an oak molding and gnawed it to bits on the carpet before I caught him.

I am sure he is still plotting ways to get the fish out of that tank. Licking them out didn't work. Chewing their house didn't work. Any projections, what is next?

Bobbi Sparr

Just out of curiosity, is this TV watching and guarding thing "standard"? I have lived with working dogs for over 20 yrs and have NEVER had a dog watch TV (admittedly, this is my first 'Dale). I am kept safe from all sorts of things. Last night he was arguing with lions; the night before we were hunting racoons; and this week alone, Sully has chased bears, wolves, and some little terriers chasing a furry toy-right off the television! I am not talking about a little alerting to the audio, but full blown, in your face "get outta my house" big Airedale barks, "Take that and don't come back!" I decided last night that

Schutzhund blind searches may be easier if I use lions instead of humans.

Fran Peck

Does any other Airedale on this list nap in such a silly way as Morgan does? When I am working in my home office, she always has to take a nap right under my chair. I mean RIGHT UNDER it. She plops down right on the bottom part of it, sticks her paws between the rollers, rests her head right on the metal legs that hold the rollers. I can't move or I'll roll right over some part of her!!

Gitte Koopmans

We spent the weekend at our little summer cabin. That's normal. It was raining. That's normal. Very much. That's normal. We beat a record-normal. (This time it was the most rainy day in June since 1851.)

Dina wanted to go out-that's normal. Put on rainwear. Forgot Dina's raincoat at home-normal. Walked in the woods for an hour and a half. Had a great time-that's normal. Except there was a hole in one of my boots, I had forgotten about. Well, that's normal. Came back with Dina extremely wet. Ran inside the living room to greet mom with the BigGrin and the BigShake-that's normal. Took off my rainwear. Looked for a towel to dry Dina. She started her usual routine with a very big grin: pressing herself between my legs. Started in front, quick turn and in from behind. After 5-6 tunnels she was drier and I felt as if I had peed at myself. And that's not normal!

Kjell Sjostrom

Thanks to everyone who offered advice about moving a dog to a new house. The suggestions I found particularly useful were: let the dog sniff the whole place when it is empty, have new I.D. ready in advance, and be prepared for some psychosomatic behavior (Toby's limp became more pronounced for a few days).

Jessica Rabin

Sharla asked about where to find ADT wallpaper borders. I have

Airedale wallpaper border all OVER the house and I bet some of you do, too! Check and see....Got that brownish SMUDGE running at about Beardheight all around the house, like a chair rail?

Gena Welch

Does anyone else vacuum their dogs? I was vacuuming tonight (hint from Heloise: sprinkle corn starch on those greasy bone/pig's ear spots, spread with scrub brush, let sit for 15 min., vacuum, and voila! grease spots are gone) and the boys were helping as usual. I ran the vacuum over their backs, especially that spot right in front of their tail, and they were in ecstasy.

Sidney Hardie

Mine line up to be "sucked up" when I am vacuuming. Emily opens her mouth and I "suck" the sides of her cheek/mouth to make a funny noise. When it is the next one's turn, she goes back to the end of the line to wait her turn again.

Ginny Higdon

Oliver used to want to bite my heavy wool sweaters to pieces. The first winter he lived here, I found two sweaters he didn't go wild about and just wore them all winter. Then I burned them. He's grown up to have more fashion sense. Last week he was ready for a walk early one day, so he brought my clothes down to the table where I eat breakfast. A subtle hint. He did a great job matching the sweater and pants.

Kate Middleton

Maggie has developed a thing for my green, terry bathrobe. Thank goodness it's full length because my legs would be full of nip marks. She has literally taken it off me! She grabs whichever part - arm, sash, front, back-and PULLS. I try not to pull too hard back because I don't want it to be a tug of war. Now the right pocket is 1/2 off. Brian has suggested I just give it to her. Tried that. Once it was on the floor with her, she IGNORED it! Go figure!

Judie Burcham

I dress business for work, jeans and sweatpants after and on weekends, but on Sundays after church, I come home and put on my favorite flannel pants to do laundry and Sunday stuff. Zoe wants to eat them! She goes nuts when she follows me in these flannel pants. With my jeans, sweatpants or other pants, no big deal, a few tastes and nibbles, but with the flannel pants she's out of control! It's actually funny! All 12 (or so) pounds of her tries to pull me down by my pants.

Kari Stielow

CHAPTER TWO

Nude Airedale Mud Wrestling and Other Classic Encounters

THE TITLE FOR THIS CHAPTER comes from an account written by Carol S. Dickinson of Alaska Rescue for the publication Rescue 911. It is reprinted here with her permission. The stories that follow are original, sometimes harrowing, and always true. They are governed by a logic that may not be immediately apparent. For instance, stripping naked in the back yard and dousing oneself with tomato sauce is not some kinky ritual but a way to neutralize skunk spray. You might need to know that some day.

Discovery of this sport has been a true highlight among the many odd events that happen in a rescue home. It came about because we had at one time four unneutered males sharing the household. Two of them did not get along and were always kept in separate parts of the house or yard. However, they were smart and had figured out how to bang on the door just the right way to pop the deadbolt.

One morning we had sent group A outdoors and group B had come in for morning love, medicines, and breakfast bones. We then retired to our bedrooms to dress. I had just removed my nightie and was grabbing my panties when group A broke through the deadbolt and re-entered our humble abode. Immediately the two males started argument number 103. Quite out of character, everybody else chose a side and we had an Airedale hurricane swirling through the dining area. Naturally, you don't wait to intervene, so I rushed to the fray-in the nude.

We had experienced several "discussions" of this nature and knew there was no murderous intention. It was all posturing and jockeying for rank in the pack. None of these arguments ever drew blood or caused a puncture. We were used to wading in among them, grabbing the culprits, and forcing them into neutral corners. I had no hesitation and waded in, grabbing females and submissive males and throwing them aside as I headed for the main combatants. They thought this was pretty good sport and just bounced back in as the whirling mass circled the room.

We had just had a rain after a long drought, so naturally every dog had rolled in mud. As they bounced around and I waded through, I accumulated layers of mud. I reached the two main instigators and grabbed their collars to shove them apart but couldn't hold them.

My son is learning disabled but I had taught him not to get between two arguing dogs, especially since the privilege of sharing his attention was often the subject of the argument. He had been taught to turn the water hose on fighting dogs. Following his training, he thought about the hose, but there wasn't one handy in the dining room. So he did the next best thing: he picked up the three-gallon water bowl and flung it directly into the fray. He hit the biggest target-me.

Now we had a Roseanne Arnold sized nude mud-covered woman with muddy rivulets gushing down onto mud-covered dogs and flushing the first layer of mud into the beige carpet. Being soggy and in a whirling mass of muddy dogs, I collected a second layer of mud. I said a few choice words. Several dogs got the message and stepped aside and the war was put to an end.

Believe it or not, no human body parts were injured and not one Airedale had a wound of any kind. Even the carpet suffered no permanent injury.

Carol Schwaderer Dickinson

Ladies, this should be posted on a weekend. Better yet, ladies, stop reading now. OK, now that I have the undivided attention of the ladies: Saturday morning I was getting ready to take a shower-I had put clean clothes and underwear out on the bed and had just gotten ready to dash into the shower (nothing on at the moment), when Merlin came into the bedroom, followed by Sarah-the-shadow, and jumped up on the bed. Sarah needed a boost up, so I put a hand behind her head, and she climbed up on the bed and settled down (there were 2 toys up there already for some reason). Well, Sarah saw my socks sitting on the bed and went over to chew them instead. So I reached over without thinking and took them away from her. And then, of course (pre-meditated planning on their parts? I don't think so-this was all Sarah's idea) Merlin wanted a good ear-rub. Oops. I took my eyes off Sarah for a moment, and I was standing at the side of the bed, in the nude. Did I mention that the top of the bed is a few inches lower than waist-high? Sarah slowly (so as to remain un-no-ticed) crawled over to my location and without warning demon-strated on a very delicate and important portion of my anatomy ex-actly what the NEEDLESOFDOOM can feel like. Wisely, I hast-ily disengaged her teeth from my anatomy and thought for a second or two about having her mouth permanently wired shut. Sheesh.

OK, ladies you an get up off the floor and stop laughing now-guys you can stop groaning-I lived and won't have permanent (physi-cal) scars. But I won't be trusting Sarah in that situation again, either. Lesson learned. Not my favorite way to become wide-awake on a Saturday morning.

Bill Austin

I have had to wrestle Teddy nude when he got us both skunked. I had to undress in the backyard and get both of us full of tomato paste and then get in the bath tub. Thank goodness for woods and country living where my neighbors couldn't see.

Geri Lowe

Nudity in 'dale owners seems to be almost the proper thing. Per-sonally I blame it on the 'dales. Misty loves to pretend to wrap herself around a tree and then wait until I am half way ready to take a bath and looking out the window to see what she is up to. Since no one else is home, I get to go out and unwind her while she sits there (unwound) and tilts that cute little head and says, "Gottya, Mom!" and I wonder just who has seen me in my underwear Will I ever learn?

D'Arlene-Anne Kapenga

Our two ADTs have been after a smallish skunk that lives somewhere on our property and saunters by our house each evening. They have figured out how to piss off the skunk and not get skunked. We have been walking the dogs on leashes at night so they won't get sprayed. Last night the skunk was waltzing past our glass sunroom and the dogs were "attacking" Ms. Skunk through the glass. Well, Ms. Skunk raised her tail and sprayed the glass! The dogs went nuts, I really thought they were going to go through this floor to ceiling glass! So I guess you could say they got "virtually skunked". Unfortunately you can smell it but it isn't as bad as it could have been.

Susan Sheehan

Jack and Riley hunt each other a lot. They race around the yard chasing and fighting when all of a sudden they both come to a sudden stop about 30 feet apart. They look like a pair of gunfighters as they stand facing off. Riley is tall and proud, his entire body drawn up, his neck arched, staring down his rather long nose. Jack looks like Low Down Sneaky Pete, his body and head low and mean. They stand and stare at each other with hard-bitten gaze, just waiting for the other guy to flinch. Jack will slowly, slowly, raise a paw, practically a toe at a time, and inch forward. This continues until finally Riley moves some muscle in his body; whereupon Jack rushes forward and the two CRASH together like two rutting stags.

Sidney Hardie

Kanako Ohara wrote: Speaking of hunting, I'm wondering if any of your 'dales share the same peculiar hunting style as Teddy. No, not the stalking, but rather the slowness of the stalking. I mean, when

Teddy stalks, she moves really, extremely S——L——O——W.

Georgia runs out our back door bark/screaming at the rabbits and birds, at about 90 M.P.H. She has caught 3 rabbits and at least as many birds. Branagan is a stealth hunter, quiet and sneaky and has caught his share of prey that way. Normally, at home, G. runs and barks, flushes the game, and B., who has not uttered a sound, just stands and waits for whatever to run past him and grabs it! True teamwork and talk about easy!

Yvonne Michalak

When my oldest son was in second grade, he wanted a pet rat. So we got a beautiful lilac-hooded one. My husband says I can never have just one of anything, and, yes, I got another. They really do make nice pets. Mike would ride his bike and his rat sat on his shoulder. Then we had a litter, so ugly they were cute, and we had an Airedale at the time. Dixie would lie by the cage and watch them constantly. I had warned Mike that should one get loose, she would probably kill it.

Then one day I saw Dixie sneaking down the hall away from Mike's room and thought "Oh no, please, no!" The cage had been pried open. Mom and babies were there-minus one. They were about three weeks old now and had hair and their eyes were open. They were almost old enough to be weaned. I went and found Dixie to scold her. She looked up at me through her eyebrows and I realized she had something in her mouth. GROSS! I said, "Drop it," and held out my hand. She opened her mouth and deposited the baby rat. Alive, unharmed, and soaking wet. She then proceeded to lick it as though it were a puppy. This from the dog that would take my sliding glass doors off the runners in her frenzied attempt to get outside and catch the squirrels that lived in the trees.

Barbara Schneider

The scene: I am washing dishes at the back window. Milo is outside sound asleep under his tree, but a little out of my sight. Otis is in the cellar cooling off. We live on an old non-working farm where lots of wild animals wander in from time to time-deer, moose, fox, raccoons, etc. As I am watching out the back window, along comes a wild turkey strutting across my back yard. I'm thinking, "Oh, Thank God Otis doesn't see him....hey wait a minute, where's Milo. Isn't he out there? Hmm, did Milo get loose? Maybe he is in the house?"

So I move to the other window where I watch the turkey strut up to Milo under the tree, check him all out, turn. Milo must have opened his eyes at this point, for the turkey quickly starts strutting away, his pace getting faster and faster and then a quick "Oh, Sh*t, I better fly."

I am thinking, "Uh oh, someone is going to have turkey for lunch." I am sure Milo is going to pounce. Next thing I know, out from under the tree into my view, comes Milo all sleepy eyed, looking around as if to say, "Hmmm. I think, Hmmm-did I dream that?" He looks around, gazes at the sky, sniffs the air, looks very bewildered, shakes his head, looks my way as if to say, "Mom, was there a bird just here?" Looks bewildered some more, and then goes back under the tree to sleep or dream some more! I was in the house in stitches laughing. All I gotta say is that bird doesn't know how lucky he is! And Otis, in the house the whole time, will never know what he missed.

Shirley Sanborn

Monty the ADT and Homer the cat have been seen hunting/stalking bugs together, despite Monty's usual habit of mouthing Homer to a sticky mess. Monty's stalking is so catlike, the idea of them hunting together doesn't seem that strange. I once watched them both, side by side, sneaking up on a ferocious beetle (maybe they'd see Starship Troopers the night before). It was all a big game between them, batting the helpless bug back and forth between their paws. That was, until Homer stopped, looked up at Monty, pounced on the bug, CRUNCH in his mouth, and jumped over the fence. Poor Monty sat there looking up at the empty fence (perhaps plotting his revenge, but more likely thinking "I thought I thaw a puddy tat").

Marc Lawrence

Dalton is a big chipmunk and squirrel hunter but one time we went camping and a bear walked down the nearby road a few hundred feet from the tent and you never saw an Airedale get to the bottom of a sleeping bag so fast!

Vicki Richards

"How do you train for the fur test? Is there written material? I have started Madie on human tracking but would love to come to the ADT hunting/working trials some day. I have wondered if her high prey drive (especially for critters) with a nose-to-the-ground style might make her suited for the fur test." Dorothy Dunn Duff

I didn't have a clue, initially, a few years ago. I took a page out of my "x's" schutzhund tracking training and started with a very short trail of raccoon scent (10 feet). You can use commercially produced raccoon scent mixed in a small bucket of water. Dunk a cloth rag tied to a short stick in the coon-coction and swab a 2-foot square patch at the start of your trail. This is your "scent pad" where you will introduce your pup to the scent. The trail, or track, leads from this pad. You will be working your 'dale on-lead, making sure they stay on the track. I started by laying the short track, placing hot dog treats at "footstep" intervals. This teaches the dog to follow the scent/treats. You will gradually wean them off of the treats, as they gain confidence. Now, this teaches "nose-down" scenting but if your 'dale is an "air-scenter" that is fine. Just be sure you are consistent with teaching them about the scent you want them to follow.

As your 'dale gains confidence, lengthen the tracks. I always put a reward at the end of the track-treats, their food, a toy, the coon cage. Make sure it's just out of reach, unless you have a coon handler to raise and lower the cage, and make darn sure you keep the coon out of reach by keeping the 'dale on lead; they can get bitten by the coon, or pull a tooth out on the cage! Make sure your shots are up-to-date! Rabies and distemper are very common coon maladies, among others. I taught them to bark by barking myself; having them around other dogs that'll bark at critters will help, too. Not all 'dales are natural critterbarkers, as some of the junior fur testers will attest to. Keep in mind that at the coon tree, some 'dales may be unsure as to what they are supposed to do. If they do bark, grumble, woof, whatever, you have to encourage it and reinforce the behavior! Don't waste the moment, because they will quit barking as soon as they start. Gentle patting of their flanks and encouragement should keep them going.

We had good timing and success at the warm-up cage on Saturday and Sunday with barking but some didn't carry over to the junior test. Don't get discouraged. The dogs are inexperienced, and a little training will produce some passing junior scores.

'Dale Burrier

I'm in New Mexico with Oscar and Madie and we were out cleaning the garage. Madie and Oscar are really into mice hunting and there are plenty to hunt around here (we are up in the mountains). Madie had already caught one and she had responded to my "drop it." I don't want them to eat their catch as there is danger of various types of infectious diseases (would rather they didn't catch them but they are terriers). Well it was Oscar's turn but he doesn't know "drop it." When he made his catch I yelled to my step-son to get it away from him (Oscar is a cairn-type, no jaws of death). But as he reached for Oscar, Oscar tilted his head up and with one big gulp: no mouse. I responded. "Oh no, I know he'll be barfing tonight." Well, in less than a minute up came the mouse STILL ALIVE. Yuck! Madie made a leap for the barfed up mouse (even grosser) but we interceded and disposed of the mouse in time.

Dorothy Dunn Duff

Jack and Riley had their own little private lure course this morning. Some cat with a death wish entered the yard. One second the guys were sitting at my side in the living room and the next second,

I heard the WHAP! WHAP! of the dog door. I got up and saw a long streak, going first one way down the fence line, then the other: cat, Jack, Riley. So far, it's cat 1, Airedales 0; but if it's smart, that cat won't push its luck. Do you know the name of some national organization I can contact to find out when they might be coursing in my area?

Sidney Hardie

Sidney, when we lived in town, our house had a dog door and all the houses in the neighborhood were built the same (tract house) and I assume most had a dog door in the same room as ours. There were a couple of nights when our wire fox terrier (WFT) would jump up on the bed to cuddle only to find a CAT was already there! Talk about chaos! One night Marly and Dalton were chasing this cat around the house and my husband (stark naked) was trying to catch the cat to put it outside unharmed. It was a very funny sight and I couldn't help him because I was laughing too hard! The next morning we realized the blinds in the game room, where most of the chasing occurred had been wide open and our neighbors to the rear usually sat out on their back porch after work (which was after 2 since they were bartenders). I imagined what they may have seen if they were up that night (we don't know if they were) was my husband running around the game room doing toe touches and high jumps stark naked while being chased by an Airedale and fox terrier!

Another time we were all watching TV in the family room while the cat haters were crashed out on the floor and couch snoozing and a cat walked right through the living room, even stepping over Dalton on his way by! My husband, calmly this time, caught the cat and put it outside then we all teased the big hunters about missing the chase of a lifetime. Now I know why my husband wanted to move where there aren't any neighbors!

Vicki Richards

When I was getting ready for bed, I faintly heard the wailing sound a chicken makes when something grabs it. I dashed downstairs and urged the dogs outside before grabbing a flashlight-a dim one because there's a rule here about never having a good working flashlight. Ran out to the chicken pen to find one hen perched outside the coop on top of a log and another at the door of the coop. Chickens awakened at light are dim bulbs, too, and very confused. I first checked them and inside the coop to make sure no predator was in there. Then, hearing Keeper's faint whine on the other end of the chicken pen, I went out and around to that side. Sure enough, there was a 'possum on the other side of the wire, still inside the coop, having been unable to find his escape route. That was fortunate, since I don't want my dogs coming into contact with a possibly rabid wild animal. So we stood there, the 'possum staring at us and the three of us staring at the 'possum. 'Possums are pretty dim bulbs, too, especially when it's night and you shine a light at them.

Keeper didn't know which was more exciting, the 'possum or the chicken wandering in the pen complaining softly and apparently unable to find its way back inside the coop. She alternated between looking at the 'possum and going over to check out the chickens. Finally Farmer John wandered down to see what was going on, by which time I was a little testy. He loped back up to the house to get a gun with which to shoot the 'possum. All this time, Darwin stood completely still and quiet, staring at the possum, which occasionally moved its head slightly back and forth. It was almost as if he were keeping it in place by watching it. I hauled him back out of the way when John came with the gun. At the first "pop," Keeper took off for the house while Darwin looked on with interest. I praised Darwin to the skies. I wonder if Keeper will ever figure out that the chickens are the ones she's supposed to protect and the varmints are the ones she's supposed to chase?

Sherry Rind

Some months ago my wife, Pia, came home from the evening walk-and was she furious. Smoke and fire poured out of her nostrils, ears and eyes. She let in the Terrible Twosome and thumped into the living room growling like bear in rage. Going out the back door, she had had to walk down some concrete stairs to the fields behind the house-but as the Terrible Twosome reached the stairs, they went berserk like they do when they see you know what. They stormed down the stairs. My wife tried to hold back the dales. But the sheer speed and power of the two pulled her out over the stair. She only hit the stairs once before crashing onto the field 12 feet below with a loud thud-whereupon the dogs got scared seeing her hit the ground and scrambled off, Nakki left and Zorba right. But my wife held onto the flexilines-and the dogs nearly pulled off her arms. And as she said: At least I saved the cat from getting mauled by the impossible dogs. By the way, she added, the cat turned out to be a plastic bag! I gave her a hug and told her she was a real hero-saving a plastic bag, risking her own life and limbs. We couldn't help laughing Well-we changed the way we walk out the back door.

Steen Selvejer

The other night at around 1:30 AM Nakki (2 years old) was whining at the door that leads from the living room to terrace and garden. His whining woke me up and I went down stairs to let him out into the garden-I thought he had to go out and relieve himself. Not so! But I was still half asleep and didn't really notice that he actually picked up a scent track-and started to track something out there-until it was too late. The scent lead him back towards the door and the terrace; in fact it lead him right up to his dog house.

I must tell you now that this dog house is something special. It was built at school by my son, Kasper-and the craftsmanship is rather impressive-but the teacher who let him build it was either misjudging the size of an Airedale or eager to save a little money and wood,'cause the dog house would do better for a Beagle (rather longish Beagle) or perhaps a Basset on a small income.

Anyway. Nakki homed in at the dog house and went absolutely ballistic. He hit the opening of the dog house like a heat seeking missile-and with a sound just like one, growling and barking in the diminutive house. The house started bouncing and dancing! I actually thought it would explode. Imagine an Airedale in fury forcing his way into a dog house way too small. I was so surprised, I didn't do anything for a second or two, then I rushed out the door to get him out from there and stop his barking, growling and fury, so he wouldn't wake up the whole village. Meanwhile he had retreated a little from the house and I then heard the cat inside of it. Nakki attacked the house and cat again, growling like the roar from a jet. I ordered him back inside our house; and much to my surprise, he backed out and went in, just like that! Zorba (9 months old) didn't dare venture out into the garden and danced the happy puppy-dance around Nakki and me as we got in. I checked Nakki-no scars or scratches-and went out to check on the cat, which was gone without leaving a trace.

The next morning I let Nakki and Zorba out into the garden, and they sniffed the garden for traces of the cat. Everything seemed calm and quiet, so I went toward the kitchen; but I didn't even get out of the living room before Nakki exploded into fury in the garden, attacking the fence, literally trying to pull the thing down with all his might. I flew out into the garden just wearing boxer shorts and nothing else (temperatures below the freezing point) to make him stop. And then I discovered that Zorba was standing on the porch of my neighbor's house where he had managed to corner the neighbor's cat! That cat normally teases Nakki and Zorba by sitting and cleaning himself or sleeping on his side of the fence, knowing for sure that he is safe no matter how hysterical the dogs behave on our side of the fence; but now Zorba was really on to him (how on earth he got in there is still a mystery) and Nakki was trying to pull down the fence.

With no time to waste, I jumped the fence and ran to the porch. Zorba got surprised, the cat got away, I got hold of Zorba, and Nakki stopped demolishing the fence. Carrying a 58 pound Airedale out of my neighbor's garden and into my house, I really woke up. My wife, though, was a little disappointed, that I hadn't started making coffee yet. I was just glad the neighbors were still asleep!

Steen Selvejer

When Judy my first ADT-mix arrived, Max the cat left for a week. Eventually Max returned and learned to live with the @#&*!@@ dog. One night after frying up chicken, I was preparing to eat when the phone rang. I dutifully answered it. When I got back to the kitchen, there was Max on the table. He had just thrown down a huge drumstick to Judy who gulped it whole while it was steaming hot. I still haven't figured out just what the cat got from the whole episode, but they made a great team. Maybe Airedales are just great persuaders.

Kent Young

Tonight while we were eating dinner, Sugar the cat came up to the table and began begging for food. She's a very brave (or foolish) kitty to do this with two Airedale bookends on each side of my chair. Bonnie was being very patient and waiting for "last bite" when Sugar got too friendly and jumped onto my lap. Believe me, Bonnie was concerned about that cat being on my lap and in closer proximity to the food than she was. Sugar turned around on my lap and waved her tail in Bonnie's face. Bonnie took the tail into her mouth and made a slight biting motion and nearly closed her mouth on the tail. It was the oddest thing I've ever seen her do. She was very careful not to actually bite down on the cat's tail. She just mimed the motion. Sugar, who's maybe not so foolish, felt the hot breath on her tail and jumped down from my lap and went to the living room. She's a lucky cat to live with an Airedale with so much self-control.

Judy Dwiggins

Gus has had a successful day hunting shrews today. I helped a little by lifting boards and things for him when he told me there was one of these little critters underneath. He was always right and he always nailed them. But they must taste bad-he always wrinkles his nose and says "E-E-E-W-W" when he kills them. Moles, possum, and raccoons don't elicit this reaction.

Barbara Mann

When Oliver was eight or nine months old, he met his first snake. To understand his reaction, you need to know that a few weeks before, he had found a used bicycle tire on one of our walks. To him, this tire was a "pearl of great price." He dragged it a good 700 yards back to the car. When we got home, he dragged it nearly 300' to the back of the yard, where it seemed to serve as some kind of totem against squirrels.

One afternoon we took our walk along a point at a nearby lake. When we reached the very tip of the point, we both saw a long black strip that looked like a bike tire in the grass. Oliver ran eagerly toward it, sniffed, then jumped back using all four feet at once-THE TIRE HAD MOVED! The tire snake then slithered into the lake. For the only time in his life, Oliver looked nervously at the world, darting his eyes suspiciously -what would come alive next? the grass? the trees? the lake? This normally cocksure puppy stood with his head down beneath his shoulders, darting his eyes. After giving him a few reassuring words, I decided to be quiet-what could I possibly do to solve such an epistemological crisis? He would have to work this one out on his own. And he did. As he walked back the car that day, he seemed to relax a bit. The next day, he dragged the bicycle tire out of the fenced part of the yard and into the driveway. He marked it well. The tire was now the first line of defense against the cat that patrolled the area around the garage.

Over the next year, Oliver seemed to remember the "tire" snake, for he repeatedly sniffed then attacked two thin black PVC drainpipes along the lake. Then one day, we tunneled through a large black pipe at a park. Oliver seemed to take special notice of it. The next time we went to the lake, he ran up to the first thin black drainpipe, gave a small sniff, and kept walking.

Kate Middleton

For years I bred and hand-fed baby cockatiels and my dogs were quite accustomed to baby birds taking their first flight, crashing into walls, falling on the floor. In fact it was often difficult feeding the baby bird because the dogs' noses were in the way. As a result my dogs are protective of our birds.

When Peter came home after his show career, I was feeding about a dozen babies. They decided to leave the confines of their basket early, and flew everywhere. Peter tracked each one and barked AT ME until I retrieved it, almost as if he were saying "Mom, there is one over here!" Then when I picked it up, he had to nose it all over to check it out before going to look for another.

Barbara Schneider

When we got our first budgie, Chewy would not voluntarily leave the side of Kelly's cage for the first couple of days. Maggie was there quite a lot too, but being a golden retriever who exists solely to play fetch, and being that Kelly was not about to throw toys for her to fetch or fly about to BE fetched, she would leave after a few minutes to find a human to throw toys for her. I would say that after a week, Chewy realized that Kelly was not going to come out of her cage and started spending less time around her, but still went running to the cage when she made any noise. After a month, even that didn't interest him that much. Now we have another budgie who can sometimes squawk very loudly and for minutes at a time and not one of the dogs will go and check on them. Probably helps that the cage hangs from the ceiling.

Barbara Osgood

Zoe treed her first raccoon! She wakened us with warning barks at 3 a.m. She was prancing at the kitchen window which overlooks the bird feeders and three fir trees and watching a raccoon that was trying to unhook one of the feeders. I let her out thinking she might give the robber raccoon a good scare. The raccoon went further up one of the trees, and Zoe went crazy circling the trees.

All was as planned until the dumb raccoon decided to come down the tree and challenge the dog. The noises as the two tangled were horrific; I panicked wondering whether 48 pound Zoe was up to the viciousness of a raccoon. Fortunately, Zoe sent the raccoon up a second tree; she turned to me and I gave the COME command. To my utter amazement, all of our practicing paid off. Before she knew what she was doing, she came! I gave her lots of praise, some rewards and locked her in the kitchen. We waited by the window, until the raccoon departed with terrific growls and whining. Zoe was not quiet. She wanted back at it. Now my question: how do Airedales fare with cornered raccoons? I do not want to sissify Zoe, but the episode has left me very apprehensive. What do I need to know?

Anne Clarke

Airedales generally kill raccoons. But that does not mean that the Airedales get away scott-free! Though the Airedale wins, they can get severely bitten, blinded, lacerated, etc.! Tally Ho has killed a coon and a ground hog, and each time I was afraid she'd be severely maimed. Raccoons are serious adversaries, and I'd rather my 'dales steer clear, than risk an eye.

'Dale Burrier

I'd say that the typical Airedale should be able to handle a raccoon. A small Airedale is still mighty, and in fact, can be faster and more agile than some of the bigger ones. That said, the part of your description that concerns me is that the raccoon decided to come down out of the tree and confront the attacking dog. This isn't usual raccoon behavior. When a raccoon really endangers itself or is toddling around during daylight hours, then I'd wonder if it has rabies or distemper, both diseases of the nervous system that promote bizarre behavior. I've heard hisses and such from treed raccoons, but the sounds coming from the animal you mention are kind of weird. As long as your dog didn't come in direct contact with the raccoon or its saliva, not to worry, provided your dog's shots are up to date.

Chris Halvorson

I still have vivid memories of my sleepy teen years, when I'd vaguely wake out of my morning stupor at the sound of the door at the end of the hall being opened and one or the other of my parents encouraging the dogs to come wake me up. The rush of however many dogs we had at the moment either resigned me to waking up or, more frequently, determined me to go back to sleep comma darnit. Unfortunately, the dogs seemed to have some sort of sixth sense about when this might happen, and the General would end up discovering my nose, eye, or ear with his drippy beard.

When I was being particularly stubborn, Dad would help the then-somewhat-aging General up onto my bed, where Gen would immediately locate my kidney with one of his paws and put all his 60+ lbs. behind it. He wasn't very keen on being on the bed, since it was squishy and put his balance off, so he would usually end up shaking the whole structure with his attempts to stay upright, then launch himself off my lower back to get to the floor.

After the General crossed the bridge, Pebbles and Talis and Joker and Gessi were more than happy to continue the service. I have misty memories of Talis bounding onto the bed-well, more particularly, onto me-with her little stiletto paws, and Pebbles generally picked up the slack with the wet beard. Joker had the long, pointy nose that managed to insinuate itself under the pillow I had usually dragged over my head: SNUFFLE SNUFFLE SNUFFLE in my ear, eye, nose, whatever. Yeah, ADTs: the natural alarm clock solution.

Jude McLaughlin

I am generally a law-abiding citizen but I ran a stop sign and almost hit a Volvo station wagon when I saw an Airedale walking with his human near my neighborhood Sunday. The man seemed a little hesitant when-after skidding through the intersection-I pulled up right next to him and rolled down my window. But he softened up when I praised his handsome 'dale, name of Barney, 7 years old and a big boy. I explained that I had an Airedale too and that I didn't see many in Houston.

Erin Blair

You may recall that last year, when Zoe was less than a year old, we tried in vain to teach her to bark at the deer in order to protect our garden of roses. (Out of five bloomings, we enjoyed only the first. The deer ate hundreds of buds and demolished the canes.) We even sought out the deer in the neighborhood and barked at them, being the best models we could be for purposeful ADT barking. (Don't laugh; barking well is harder than you think.) The only result of our efforts was that we embarrassed Zoe! She gave us that unmistakable look of: "Your behavior is sooooo embarrassing; couldn't we just go home now."

Well, guess who is now doing a grand job of keeping the deer away from the roses? Zoe, from her night-place in the kitchen, is proudly barking every time a deer approaches the garden. We leap out of bed and run (make that stumble) to the kitchen to praise and treat her for doing such a good job. At first, when we left windows on the other side of the kitchen open as well as those on the rose garden side, she "protected" us from mice, chipmunks, crickets and raccoons, as well. We took turns all night rushing to reward deer protection. Now, she is warning us only when the deer come for roses and raccoons come for bird feed. We are very proud of her and very appreciative. The roses are the best ever, and we are saving a lot of money on bird feed!!

Hugh and Anne Clarke

I've always thought my Teddy Bear Necessity was a potential killer. She is a terrier after all, and that's almost programmed into her genes, right? And this girl is also so intense when it comes to chasing things: squirrels, rabbits, pigeons, horses, cars, boats, as long as it moves. But now, I'm not so sure if she is so much a killer as she is a chaser.

We had two encounters with two different furry critters here in Manhattan. Dogs can be off leash until 9 a.m. in NY, so we go to the boat basin area alongside of Hudson River because it's a pleasant breezy walk and there are tons of dogs. Last weekend was very pleasant until Russell (the human) started to emit some unintelligible panicky stutters with his arms waving different directions and his hand pointing at something directly left of us. While I didn't understand his language, Teddy understood it perfectly and found what he spotted: a CAT!

Teddy pounced on it and cornered the poor cat against the wall before I could react. (When I later asked Russell why he didn't react before trying to tell me, he said, "I dunno. Mommy has more authority over her." Men!) The image of the poor cat hanging from Teddy's mouth with a broken neck flashed before my eyes, and I shrieked "TEDDDDY, NOOOOOO!" while lunging forward to grab a hold of her. Fortunately, my scream and the cat's desperate paw punch startled Teddy, and she backed off an inch and looked back with a perplexed expression of "now what am I supposed to do?" The cat quickly disappeared into the nearby bush. I was pleasantly surprised that Teddy didn't instantly go for the kill and also that she didn't pursue the cat into the bush. She looked very interested and searched around for the cat she lost, but when we said no, she didn't insist.

Then this morning Teddy suddenly pulled me on the leash with mighty force for about 15 feet. What did she find? Another cat!! This cat was tougher, though, because he punched Teddy and hissed at her. When I pulled her back, this cat actually took a few steps forward toward us looking all big and threatening. We stepped back, and he stepped forward again! Teddy didn't quite know what to make of it, so she looked at me with another "now what?" look. So I dragged her and fled the scene before the cat attacked my Airedale.

Kanako Ohara

CHAPTER THREE

The Airedale Gourmet

WARNING: the faint of heart or stomach may find some of the following stories too graphic. This warning will not, of course, apply to people who live with Airedales. Most of them can watch a dog vomit something disgusting beside the dinner table and calmly go on eating, unless they are compelled to clean up the carpet immediately.

Talk about stubborn, my Zak and I just went through a major battle of wills. It all has to do with food. My usually good eater decided he didn't want to eat his food in the normal way any longer. It got to the point where he would not eat unless his food was put in his Buster cube or his Kong. I had his Kong dropped on my feet and in my lap, thrown from amazing lengths across the room. Then came the Buster cube hurling across the floor. This went on for about three days.

I refused to put any food into his toys and he got extremely upset with me and totally turned his nose up at his food dish. Talk about being vocal-they sure have a way of letting you know when they think they are unjustly treated. Finally this morning he ambled into the kitchen without a toy, looked at me as if to say, "You are such a meanie, Mom," and ate. When we left for work, he was pouting in his chair just like my kids used to do when they were small. But at least I know I won this battle. Wonder what tonight will bring?

Carole Litwiller

I got home from work and decided to check my e-mail. Slow day, only 102 messages. I thought because it was only 5:00 dinner could wait. Kiai, my 10 yr. old, came over and sat at my feet so I scratched her head while I read. She left and went and rattled her food dish. I laughed, and told her in a few minutes; she came back and sat down next to me. Few minutes later, the same thing. I did not get up, just laughed again. Next she dragged the dish across the kitchen floor. I have the double SS diner. She spilled some water but still I kept reading. By now she was mad; when she came over and sat down and I tried to scratch her head she pulled away. Went over to her bowl and managed to lift it off the stand and brought it over and dropped it at my feet. Would you say this dog is food motivated? I laughed so hard but I did have to get up and feed the three of them. They are so strong willed and hard headed. Who has who trained?

Barb Oimas

While I was busy bundling up 12+ bags of garbage (once in a hundred years cleaning), Oliver opened the fridge and set up a nice buffet for himself and Music. He wisely hit all the food groups-roast beast, stuffing, butter and salad. They seemed to have moved to the living room for their dessert-pastry. My guess is we'll all be up come 2 am for the outcome of this soiree.

Kate at "Oliver's Restaurant," Middleton

If they will eat socks, what else will they eat? Well, for starters:

Annie-2 bars of soap when she was pregnant, some she threw up, some she passed through.

Eliza-socks, dishcloths, large parts of the tea towel, face cloths.

CB-last night it was the edges and handle of a stiff nylon bag that I used for cassette tapes; a couple of weeks ago it was part of one of my bras (then after she pooped it out & the rain rinsed it off, she brought it back in for me).

Catherine-many years ago ate a 6' nylon leash minus the snap and she kept it in her stomach for 3 months, then threw it up all in one piece (it went in a bright pink and came out a mottled brown).

Emily-various rocks (which thankfully came back up eventually and didn't get stuck going through); pieces of drainage pipe which had sharp edges, making her occasionally throw up bloody vomit until I remembered someone's remedy of cream-soaked cotton balls which cover the rough edges and allow it to pass through.

Philly-years ago, she ate the heel from a large squeaky boot and it got stuck; she had a rough time for a couple of days, then finally passed it (yes, I do know the dangers here).

One litter of pups-years ago ate a good portion of the fender of my big Blazer and redesigned the wheel-well of my fiberglass Boler trailer that was parked in the same yard as the puppies were kept.

Pinky-she always stuck with the edibles like a very large zucchini from the counter; potatoes from the covered storage bin; anything from any part of the counter (at a friend's place she managed to get up on the counter and walk the length of it to get what she wanted). Once she climbed out of a pen in the basement while I was out, came upstairs to the groceries that I had not yet put away and got a large bag of M&M peanuts (I know-chocolate is toxic), apples, bread, pizza crusts. The funny part of the pizza crusts was that she took them back downstairs and climbed into the pen where her son Spike was to share them with him and that is where she was when I got home.

Ginny Higdon

This reminds me of when I was single, living at the beach with four dogs. I had one, Lulu, who could open anything. I even had to resort to spring loaded eye hooks on the cupboard where the dog food was kept or she would get in there and set a picnic for the others. She could open the fridge and jump up on the counters in the kitchen and clear out anything that looked good to eat on the first couple of shelves all around. Then she and the others would lie blissfully around the house passing doggie farts that literally turned the air purple in a fog around them. She would open up gates of dog runs and let every one out-she was a monster (but I mean that in a nice way *!@#$$!!).

After a particularly stressful week or so of not being able to keep her out of anything, and having my friends jokingly tell me that one day I would come home and find that I was overdrawn at the bank, and that when my bank statements came in, checks would be signed with a paw print and Lulu and the gang would be vacationing in Cabo, I had my boyfriend, a very dry-humored Englishman engineer, come over to help me solve the problem of keeping Lulu from opening the dog door when she and the other culprits were put out for a while. Sydney actually brought his slide rule over and sat and measured and calculated for about thirty minutes. Finally he looked at me and said, in his delightfully British way, "We can do either of two things: We can dig a 400' pit in front of the door, or we can cut off their bloody arms at the shoulders!"

Obviously, we did neither! But, boy, I can remember being tense every day when I opened the door to come home from work, just waiting to see what they had "accomplished" that day while I was gone!

Terry Beyerle

Barnaby spent the day at the vet's today. Since I couldn't feed him in the morning, I waited and fed Mattie when I got back home. She didn't eat all of her food since Barnaby was not there to check and see if she had left any. She really prefers just to snack all day. When it was time to pick up Barnaby, I asked her if she wanted to go and get him. She cocked her head and looked at me, so I asked her again. She immediately went to her dish, finished off all of her food and then went to the door and looked at me to say she was ready to go now!

Maureen Phelan

I can always tell when my AireWaldo boy is eating something he shouldn't because my Golden Girl Sadie runs and gets in the crate to hide from the loud voice which will come from me. This happened yesterday when I came home from grocery shopping and put away all the groceries-or so I thought. Waldo surfed the countertop way in the back and managed to grab a large cantaloupe, carry it into the dining room (carpeted-making a mess in the kitchen is no fun) and proceed to chow down. This all happened in 5 seconds flat. He loved that sweet fruit and was not repentant in the least, still trying to grab it out of my hands as I was cleaning it up.

Rita Ferrer

I have children who think I spoil Bonnie and Beau. They sort of accept the fact though; they know they can't change me. Luckily, both daughter-in-law and future daughter-in-law had the good sense not to remark on the fact that when we were trying to get the turkey and trimmings on the table, we had 3 women, 2 men and 2 dogs all in my very small kitchen at the same time. It was a wonderful day! The two dogs were lying in the middle of the floor, Bonnie being closest to the stove, of course. We all had to dodge each other while trying not to trip over Terriers. Bonnie is so funny; she accepts women in the kitchen but the minute my husband or one of my sons walks in, she gets up and runs to stand in front of the turkey. It's like she assumes women have the duty of preparing her food and are no threat. Men, on the other hand, just come into the kitchen to steal her meal. I did put the dogs out the back door when we started eating and only let them in when we were almost finished.

When they were at last allowed in to join our dinner, Bonnie went around the table and checked each person's plate to see who had food left. The "food on plate" person became her target for begging. She's very good. She lays her head on your knee and looks up worshipfully at the plate of food. Beau sits a safe distance away from the table (out of reach of the "wrath of Bonnie") and looks adorable. He begs by raising one paw as if to say "Please!" He has very nice manners. I guess these two young women are keepers, though. I didn't hear one word from either of them about it not being sanitary to have dogs in the kitchen or that dogs don't belong on the furniture.

Judy Dwiggins

I dropped a Satsuma orange on the floor and Darwin snatched it up. The Satsumas are extremely sour this year, so I didn't think he'd eat it. He walked over to the family room and bit down. His eyes opened a little wider and he dropped the orange, dripping juice. I went to get it but he grabbed it and we did a game of chase around the downstairs (something I would not do if I were seriously trying to take something from him; he knows he has to come to me in those cases). Whenever he dropped the sour orange, I made a feint toward it and he picked it up again and ran.

I had to get back to cooking dinner, so I called all the dogs over to the treat jar and made everybody sit. Tracy got a treat, then Keeper got a treat, then Darwin ran away with his orange! I had to call them all over again and this time Darwin finally traded the orange, which he definitely didn't want to eat, for a treat. (Extra report: The two-legged kid got a haircut today. I don't know what the hairdresser put on it but when he sat on the couch, Keeper came up behind him and began licking his head.)

Sherry Rind

Several years ago I made bird feeder type decorations to put on an outdoor tree. Two little girls and I worked hours stringing popcorn, mushing seeds into peanut butter encrusted pine cones. You guys get the picture. Then we all trooped outside, decorated the tree and stood back to admire our handiwork. Then I said, hold on, let me get the camera! Well, you know what happened. In the time it took me to get into the house and back outside again the tree was stripped bare and two very guilty ADT's were just finishing off the popcorn strand!

Patti Larrabee

My lovely federal blue carpet has been decorated with splotches of red. Seems Ellie was fascinated by the artificial pomegranates I'd laid in a chair, waiting to adorn the mantle and the Nativity figurines for a little bit o' Christmas. She left the greenery, and I did learn what those artificial pomegranates are made of-Styrofoam and lots of red stuff! I did watch for any signs of gastric distress since this happened. HAS to have been Ellie, as there have been none. She is the family Dispose-All.

Gena Welch

My first Airedale Sally loved roadkill. It was always a contest to see whether I could move her away from it before she snarfed it up. Once we were walking along a private gravel road and she grabbed the remains of a dead squirrel. She stayed just out of my reach as she gulped the necessary times to swallow it. All that was left sticking out of her mouth was the fuzzy gray end of the tail. When I finally caught her I grabbed the tail end of the squirrel and brought it up the way it went down. As usual with these incidents she was none the worse for it.

Mary Giese

Our old ADT, Zeus, was fond eating lots of things. The most memorable was my father's wedding ring. My father followed Zeus around for days waiting for the inevitable to take its course, and it did. And after a careful washing, the ring was none the worse for wear! Zeus also ate a 22 caliber bullet that I had dropped. He retrieved it and swallowed without chewing it, thank god. This time however we stayed completely away from his rear until he passed it in his stool. We were hoping he would not shoot anyone when he went to the bathroom! I mean how would you explain that to the police; they would never believe you. I can see headlines now, "AIREDALE TERRIER TAKES DUMP AND SHOOTS OWNER BETWEEN THE EYES. IT WAS A LUCKY SHOT POLICE SAID."

Alan J. Wilson

Thelma started using Charlie to fetch her canned goods shortly after I brought him home as a puppy. She would chew through can and all to get the contents. I ended up putting a gate between the kitchen and pantry to keep her out. I returned home one day after a brief outing to find the remains of Thelma and Charlie's scavenging. There were cans of peas, corn, soup of all varieties in a steady stream from the pantry to my Oriental rug where embedded in the nap were the remains of what I think may have been a can of chili. Tuna fish was just beginning to be devoured as I entered the house. I couldn't believe the mess but had to giggle at what the sight must have been of those two working together to make their own dinner.

Bobbi Sparr

Winston got a coffee bean off the floor a couple of weeks ago when I was pouring them into the grinder. I expected him to spit it out, but he crunched it right down and wagged his tail wanting more! Now every morning when I am making coffee, he stands next to me and stares at the floor, ready to pounce on a wayward bean. He seems to prefer Starbucks-I guess he is a true Seattle dog!

Laurie Matthews

Most dogs seem to take in water loudly, lustily, and with no rhyme nor reason. Aurora, on the other hand, always drank very daintily, in 2, 3 ,4 or 5 metre, with no splashes (Teddy is a huge splasher!). I teach music lessons on Wednesdays, and we always watched for Aurora to pass by the piano on the way to her water bowl, and then we listened: drink, drink...drink, drink...drink, drink, drink...drink, drink, drink...drink, drink, drink, drink, drink...drink, drink, drink, drink drink ... and so on. It was always rhythmical and had patterns. The kids used to come in, listen to discover if anyone was at the water bowl, and then identify the dog by the rhythm, or lack thereof! A seventh grade boy mentioned it the other day, saying that he missed hearing Aurora refresh herself, and asked, "Does Teddy have rhythm?" Are there any other "Rhythmic Refreshers" out there?

Janice Tucker

My female, Cooper, has her own method of getting her first drink in the morning. When my husband gets up and goes into the bathroom, Cooper is waiting next to the tub. He turns on the faucet and she drinks until he is ready to turn the hot water on and the shower. Sometimes, we can even coax her to stand in the tub and drink. It is amazing to us how much she drinks!

Amy Turner

I think Red will beat them all. You give him two or even more very big bowls of water. He changes from one bowl to the other, "eating" the water. And you can collect the money of the spectators. Yes, we did it at the dog school. After that we had a drink too with the collected money.

Jeanine Dara

I noticed that the number of goldfish in my pond was steadily diminishing. Couldn't imagine what was happening to them until I noticed Havoc on the patio playing with one. I had known that he loved playing in the pond, destroying waterlilies and getting himself wet enough so that large quantities of soil adhered to his feet and whiskers, then personalizing my carpeting and countertops with big black footprints; but who could imagine that he would teach himself to fish? His talent for destruction is only surpassed by his infinite charm-luckily for him.

Jean Wilson

All right you puppy owners who are thinking about teaching your dog a cute trick, PAY ATTENTION! I once saw another owner and dog do this and thought it was cute so I taught Tigger, he being the food-oriented one. Last night I was getting into bed with a cup of tea in one hand, a book in the other and a homemade biscotti in my mouth with most of it (the biscotti) hanging out. As I put the tea down on my nightstand, threw the book on the bed and started to pull back the covers, up onto the bed so very gently jumps Tigger. Now Tigger, bless his heart, rarely does anything gently. He is gentle with Jacob and his young friends, but basically Tigger is a big galumphf! So I knew trouble was brewing. Tigger gently reached his long neck over and took a bite of my biscotti! He did leave me some and never came close to my mouth, but he had only done this trick with a dog biscuit or cheese before. It was pretty funny. And of course Sadie saw the entire scene, so being the good mother (or was it the good witch?) that I am, I gave Sadie the remaining piece that

I was holding with my teeth! Then I went back to the kitchen and got another biscotti in my hand. It was pretty funny to see this big black nose right by my mouth and he was gentle.

Abbe Stashower

In my back garden I have two ornamental pear trees. The trees produce tiny pears not much bigger than small grapes. Occasionally I see the birds eating these fruits. In the recent deep-freeze and thaw, the fruit has gotten very mushy and some has fallen to the ground. Targa has been picking it up from the snow and eating it. Obviously it is to her liking, because she can no longer wait for it to fall to the ground. She positions herself under the tree, and leaps up until she is completely air(e)born and in mid-air she plucks the tiny fruits from the tree with her front teeth. Quite a show! She jumps and jumps and jumps, each time picking a tiny fruit off the tree.

Gitte Koopmans

I am the proud new owner of Miles, a rescue'dale from Ohio. He will be 6 yrs old 4/2/99. This is the 4th ADT to let me share a house with him, so the cleverness of ADTs is no surprise to me. Miles, his first day in our home, busted into the fridge twice. I watched him watch me work the fridge door. I became afraid. Rightfully so it seems. He has repeated this trick 4 times. Once right in front of me on a different fridge in our house up north. Boy did I scold him! We have bungee corded the door of the fridge; but I am still afraid. You see, Miles also knows how to open doors that are merely closed with a door knob and regular latch! Locks? The Velcro closure we put on the fridge doors did nothing to stop him. We had to go to heavy duty bungee cords. For all I know, Miles is probably a safe cracker while we nap at night!

Kirk Nims

Today I was in a domestic mood and made a double batch of banana bread. The two loaves were on the counter cooling for most of the afternoon. Charlie came home from school and we let Ziggy out to pee. Behind my back I heard a clatter! I turned to find Jake starting to leave the kitchen with an entire loaf of banana bread in his huge jaw. In a flash I had it out and back on the counter. Jake did get the little chunk out of the top, but the bread is otherwise intact. Now, my question to the panel is: would you or would you not go ahead and eat this loaf of banana bread anyway?

Stephanie Coulshaw

(Editor's note: The list voted a unanimous "yes.")

I decided to be neighborly and make a cake for one of my closest neighbors. She has a huge feast at her home every year and feeds an army of family. She has been a little under the weather so I decided to make something special for their Easter gathering. My day did not go anything like what I had planned, but my heart was in the right place. I saved a recipe from last year for a Pineapple & Cherry Upside Down cake and thought that would make a nice Easter presentation. Everything was coming together nicely and the house had a wonderful aroma of just baked cake. Delicious I thought, until the catastrophe.

My UPS man was at the front door and I was thankful because I have been nervously awaiting an important package. Kugel was going totally nuts to be the first down the steps to bark at and greet my delivery guy and in a total Airedale burst of energy, she managed to knock me into the granite countertop. Trying to balance myself from an unexpected sideswipe, I managed to catch the cake rack with my elbow and the cooling cake was sent flying up into the air and Splat down onto the floor. I couldn't believe what had just happened nor could I believe the package I have been waiting for is still not here! When I went back upstairs to the kitchen floor, I could not help but notice more than half of the cake had mysteriously vanished and one particular Airedale was dribbling pineapple and cherries from her mouth! All of my hard work for nothing other than an Airedale snack? Next time, Kugel will be outside on her lead before I attempt another bake-off.

Kiwi Karley

I'd like to remind you of a quick home remedy if your dog(s) ingest chocolate: A repeated dose of 1 tablespoon of hydrogen peroxide until they vomit. Doesn't work on every dog, all the time. My late Cody once ate a 2 LB bag of Hershey Kisses (most with the foil wrappers). The vet had me start the peroxide. An entire bottle later (she had monitored this by phone so I knew I wasn't over dosing him)-nada. Had to take him in where they gave him the charcoal and still-nada. He was sent home all wags and his usual kisses, albeit complete with a black tongue! The vet's Lab had done the same thing at Christmas with the same end result. We were convinced these guys had stomachs of steel!

Judie Burcham

The Pumpkin Diet for Overweight Dogs, courtesy of Chris Zink. Reduce your dog's regular food by 25 to 33 percent, and replace that amount with twice as much canned pumpkin (not pie mix, just plain pureed pumpkin). For example, if you are currently feeding your dog three cups of food per day, you would instead feed him two cups of food and two cups of canned pumpkin. Feeding twice a day (AM and PM) may also decrease hunger. Measure your dog's food in a measuring cup; don't guess at it. Read more at http://www.CANINESPORTS.com/ and look under Articles & Book Excerpts.

Sidney Hardie

CHAPTER FOUR

Heroes and Therapists

WHILE FEW DOGS are as heroic as the Fornellis' Winston, whose stories also appear in the previous book, every Airedale has his or her moments of surprising insight, courage, or just plain stubborn insistence that he knows something you do not. Along with a stubborn willingness to stand up to anything-unless it is a truly threatening plastic bag-the Airedale shows enough steadiness and empathy to make an excellent therapy or assistance dog.

You wrote about our Winston and how special he must have been. Since he died we have never gone a day without thinking about him. We feel guilty for not realizing he was a "once in a life time" dog while he was still with us. We were so ignorant when we got him that we just thought all Airedales were like him. (What would you expect from folks who did not even know his tail should have stood up?) We experienced more with Winston in any given year of his life than with all the rest of our dogs put together. That dog could open any door, turn bolt locks, roll down car windows and when we finally had a sliding glass door he could not open, he rang the door bell. He once attacked a 1/2 ton pick-up head on as he thought Grandpa was a stranger driving off with daughter Suzanne.

He was the best the breed had to offer and the irony is he should have been put to sleep at birth. The breeder sent us a sick puppy knowing we would not know the difference. Two days after we had Winston, our vet recommended we put him down. Can you imagine what we would have missed?

Winston came into our family when Suzanne was 3 1/2 years old and her sister Angela was 9 months. Winston seemed to know these were his girls and looked after them against the world, which at times included us. If I was angry with the girls for some reason, he would bunt me from behind with his big bone head. I got very used to scolding my daughters as I was being butted from the room. When Angela graduated from a crib to a jr. bed, she discovered freedom. One night I was escorting her up the stairs and back to bed for the umpteenth time and at the top stair gave her a smack on her well-padded, double cloth diapered behind. The next thing I knew, I was flying backwards down the entire flight of 13 steps. Winston had grabbed the flared bottom of my jeans.

I have never forgotten how that dog had his tailed curled between his legs and was shaking in the face of my anger. Nor have I forgotten how he got between me and the stairs, barring my way until I had calmed down. We never had a worry about the safety of our "babies" as long as Winston drew breath.

I came to trust Winston completely. Many, many times his instincts about people proved correct. The first time he showed protectiveness was one evening when the children and I were alone, a salesman came to the door. Winston, then 10 months old, would not allow me to open the door without him going through first. Getting rid of the "salesman," by telling him through the closed door to go away, I later heard he was arrested for pushing his way into a home, frightening the family and robbing them. There was also a friend of ours who seemingly adored Winston but the dog would not allow this person near the girls or me if Bob was not present. It became a joke among our group. It was no joke when a year after we moved from the town, that same "friend" kicked his chained dog to death.

The most interesting event took place when we were selling our home. At the time we had McGuire. The sales agent brought a fellow to see the property. McGuire stood his ground at the gate, only allowing the agent to pass. Sheba, my daughter's little Yorkie mix, dashed under the big dog's legs and nipped the fellow's ankles. I managed to get the prospective buyer past the dogs only to be confronted by my pet horse, Kootney, in whose opinion this man was not to be allowed in the house. At this point, I was inclined to agree with the animals and told the agent I was sorry but the situation was impossible. I still think there was something not quite right with that man.

Amymarie & Robert Fornelli

When Brodie was just under 2 years old, I had just started dating a friend of a friend of a friend. Being a single woman living alone, I didn't let him pick me up at home until about the fourth date. When he picked me up, I told him to wait in the car as I didn't want to get Brodie all worked up over a new friend and then leave him. He was fine with this, although he kept telling me how excited he was to meet Brodie someday. When he dropped me off that night, he asked to come in for a few minutes. Since he seemed to be harmless, I said okay. Good thing I did or who knows how long he would have been around. Brodie approached this new friend in his usual "hi there, wanna play ball" mode, with his entire body going 100 miles per hour. Upon closer inspection, he dropped the ball, the hackles went up, and Brodie backed up until he walked into me, then proceeded to stay between me and this guy. After about 10 minutes of this, I told the guy that he needed to leave before Brodie got really upset. Next time he called for a date, I turned him down. I trust Brodie more than I trust my gut when it comes to judging people's character.

Diane Maxwell

Banjo is my assistant whenever I'm meeting new real estate clients or in an area that I'm not too sure about. A few years back, I met some clients at a ranch that was 50 miles from here. The people were a little strange and Banjo really didn't like the look or feel of them. He sat in the front seat and did his Airedale Clint Eastwood glare at them. All went all right and as I drove down this long road out in the boonies, I was really glad my "assistant" was with me. He can't type or answer the phone, but as a body guard he excels!

Ann Erickson

When my husband Saul, son Jacob, and I ran in the University of Washington's Dawg Dash, we brought the dogs to run with us. It was great fun, until we went past the football stadium. The UW's mascot is a Husky! Right in front of the stadium is a statue of a Husky. Tigger stopped short in his tracks, puffed himself up, sized up the other "dog" and started to spar (or try to)! Saul had run ahead with Jacob and it was up to Sadie and me to get this goof-ball of an Airedale off and running again. Like Beau; he wasn't ready to leave until he had taken this one down. And like Bonnie, Sadie paid no attention to it, except to roll her eyes at Tigger!

Abbe Stashower

Tonight I was walking Beau along our same old route and passed a house that we always give a wide path to because a mean-sounding dog lives there who bites at us through the fence. This time the owner was with his dog in the front yard, but it was loose. They were visiting with another dog and its female owner. The other dog was a pit bull. The pit bull took one look at Beau, slipped out of the man's grip, and ran straight at Beau. The second dog started running toward us, too. The owners were yelling for the dogs to come back and I was screaming "No, NO, NO, NOOOO!" I aimed my squirt bottle of vinegar-water at the pit bull's face and squeezed the trigger. Luckily my bottle was set at the long distance squirt and hit the dog in the nose at about 20 feet. The pit bull looked like, "YIKES, that's terrible stuff!" He swerved and ran right passed us. I then squirted the husky/wolf mix who stopped in its tracks and ran back into the yard. I'm so glad I learned about vinegar spray on the list. I used to carry pepper spray but I don't know if I ever would have used it. I don't want to seriously harm an animal when its stupid owners are the ones to blame for letting out of control dogs loose in an unfenced area.

I told the guy as he was pulling his dog back into the yard, "Don't worry, it's only vinegar and water." At least he had the sense to mumble "Sorry about that." My knees were shaking for the next two blocks. Beau didn't even bark when the dog attacked. I couldn't believe it-when I yelled "No" at the pit bull, I yanked Beau behind me, grabbed the bottle and stood with my legs spread apart, ready to jump on the dog if the spray didn't work. It's really lucky the vinegar spray worked because I probably would have been seriously injured trying to pull that dog off Beau-not to mention what that dog would have done to Beau. It was a large pit bull. All the way home Beau kept looking up at me and smiling. He looked very grateful and relieved that I had protected him.

By the way, someone asked me the other night about the mixture of vinegar and water I use. I didn't measure the last time I made it, but I'd say it has about 1/3 vinegar to 2/3 water. It's pretty strong-it's brownish colored in the bottle. I don't use it on Beau. All I have to do is squirt the bottle toward the ground and he settles down.

Judy "Annie Oakley" Dwiggins

Monty is just a puppy (7 months old) and loves everyone and gets all jumpy/bouncy/happy when anyone or anything new comes to the house. So much for having some element of guard dog, right? Apparently wrong. After heading off for work this morning, we remembered we hadn't locked the side gate. Went back to lock the gate and stuck a hand through the opening beside the gate. Now Monty has done the occasional BIGBADBARK when he's heard people out the front, but mostly he is just curious. Well when I opened the gate, from the other side of the yard was roaring this black & tan cannonball (not on the tips of his toes as I thought he would, but low to the ground and tucking those long legs up under his body in a blur of forward motion). There was a growl/woof coming from the depths of his chest that made the ground tremble. And here's me standing slackjawed at the gate thinking "please recognize me, please, please, please." Finally got it together to open my mouth and say "Okay, good boy" (just anything really) and he doubled in height, halved his speed, and went into his happy-prance-tip-of-the-toes walk and gave me his normal greeting of an attempted snap at my crotch. BUT, he did insist on having a look out the open gate first, thinking, something must be out there other than you, otherwise why would I have barked?

Marc Lawrence

My daughter loves mylar balloons with helium in them. She currently has a Pooh one that is losing it momentum and now is about 21/2 feet from the floor. It just kind of hovers. Last night it made its way into the bedroom. We turned off the TV and suddenly Dakota jumped straight up from his lying position at the foot of the bed, let out his most ferocious bark and immediately backed up until he was ON our heads. It took a minute to figure out that he was barking at the balloon hovering at the foot of the bed. My fearless, brave boy! He 'bout gave us a concussion trying to get away from it! But this morning he grabbed the balloon and shook it furiously. It is now deflated, dead, and we are all safe and sound, thanks to Kota.

Linda Taylor

A few weeks ago we got new neighbors, five acres away, and on their first night in their home Dalton and our OES, Bridget, would not stop barking! Our sheepdog, being a puppy, occasionally barks at coyotes, but for Dalton to interrupt his beauty sleep is almost unheard of. My husband and I yelled at them umpteen million times and finally they went to sleep after about four hours. All we could figure was that the neighbors' dogs were barking at all the new country noises and our dogs were barking at the new dogs. The next morning as I was leaving for work, I saw all my flowers had been pulled from the pots and thrown around the porch but not eaten. I cussed at all the bunnies and wondered why they all of a sudden wrecked all my flowers when the flowers had been there for three months already! The answer to this mystery? Our horses had gotten loose during the night (hubby didn't lock the gate-again)! Being almost dogs themselves, the horses spent the night on the porch looking in the windows trying to tell us they were out.

Then they trotted down the driveway and got around the fence where they could see their corral but not get to it. When my husband went to feed them, he saw them over the fence. He got a rope and two halters and walked around to get them, thinking he would have to rope and halter them; but as soon as they saw him they ran up to him, so glad to see him, and followed him home unhaltered! So Dalton and Bridget were barking for a good reason! They ended up being heroes.

Vicki Richards

Mr. Keeper and I are out for our long weekend walk and come across a little boy (about 8, I'd guess) playing with his dogs in his yard. One of the dogs, (10 pounds & 10 inches tall, tops) comes charging out in the road snarling and barking at us. The little boy yells for Squeaker to get back in the yard. Squeaker has his own agenda, so keeps charging Keeper (77 pounds at his last vet visit).

Now, Keeper loves everybody, and dogs especially, so he's bouncing around trying to play with the little dog. I'm worried he's going to smack the little dog with one of his bear paws and hurt it. The little boy comes out in the road still yelling at Squeaker to get back in his yard. I tell him not to worry, that Keeper just wants to play and won't hurt his dog. He tells me, "You'd better watch it, lady, or my dog will tear yours up; he likes to bite!" Thankfully Keeper and I made it home without further incident.

Linda Cunningham

This reminds me of a "fight" that my first Airedale, Sally, was in. Due to the incompetence of the handlers, we ran our dogs into each other while practicing the finish on lead. The other dog, a young Jack Russell Terrier, took it quite personally and attacked Sally. He jumped on her back and had a good hold on the scruff of her neck. Since he was only about half grown, he wasn't inflicting any damage, or any apparent pain. Since he was a terrier, he didn't let go until his handler pried him loose. Sally thought it was all a terrific game and wanted to play again. She got in the classic play position, with her chest on the floor and her butt up in the air, tail wagging so fast you couldn't see it. The Jack Russell wanted another go, too, but he wanted blood, so we humans decided to end the game. Sally saw that dog every week at obedience class, and would immediately start wagging her tail.

Chuck Booher

A little over a year ago, we had some severe weather in Atlanta. I am a computer geek, and typically work until well after 1:00 AM on my system at home over a line to my office. This night there had been a tornado, so I decided to stay up and work a little later than usual just in case. About 1:15 the announcer came on the radio and said that a tornado had touched down in Sandy Springs (a section of Atlanta) and was headed due east at 50 MPH. This was not good. I live about 5 miles east of Sandy Springs. I looked at Merlin, who had parked himself next to my chair, and said, "Come on, Merlin, we're going to the basement."

Merlin stood up as I was speaking (I was still seated) and grabbed my left arm in the JAWSOFDEATH and started pulling me toward the basement as hard as he could (I had teeth marks the next day). I said, "No, Merlin, we've got to go get Mommy and Nicholas! Go get Mommy! Go get Nicholas!" He ran to the upstairs bedrooms, barking at the top of his lungs. He ran into our bedroom, jumped on the bed with Cathy, and barked a few times in her face to wake her up. He then jumped out of bed and ran into Nicholas' bedroom, still barking, where he tried to jump up to the upper bunk bed to get Nicholas. By this time I had gotten up the stairs and had told Cathy about the tornado. She got out of bed and I headed for Nicholas' room. I told Merlin to get Mommy, and I got Nicholas out of bed. Merlin ran to our bedroom and grabbed Cathy's sleeve and started tugging her toward the stairs.

We all made it safely to the basement, but during our way downstairs, the tornado took a turn and went about 600 yards south of us, leveling everything in its path. At this point, Merlin waited until we were downstairs, then went upstairs to get a drink and some food. He then came back down, wagging, as if to say, "What in the world are you guys doing down here in the basement-there's nothing going on outside any more." Just to be safe, we waited until the radio had said the tornado had passed before we returned to bed. This was, by the way, the worst tornado to hit Atlanta in over 75 years, and we had many friends and acquaintances whose property was damaged or destroyed.

Bill Austin

We are on vacation in North Carolina without our furkids, so we had to wake ourselves up this morning. No Chester poking his nose in my face, no Hanna leaping on to the bed and dropping a soggy tennis ball on my pillow. Being up here again reminded us of our trip last spring with the dogs. One of our stops was at an outlet mall. While Judith went in to shop for supplies, I walked the dogs and then sat on one of the benches outside the store. I tied the dogs to the bench, which seemed like a good, solid object, while I went back to the car to get something.

Returning, I saw an older gentleman walking toward the waste basket that sat at the opposite end of the bench from the dogs. Chester stood there in his best stance with the gentleman fixed in his unwavering stare. Hanna, ever the cautious one, took a step back and lowered her head but kept her sights on the approaching stranger. I quickened my pace but not fast enough. The gentleman figured the best course of action was to keep his distance and throw the trash at the can. The trash, an empty plastic bag, was immediately caught by the wind and blown directly at my two young ADTs. Their reaction was to chose flight over fight against this unknown foe, like a sled dog team dragging this iron and wood bench across the parking lot, being chased by an empty bag and a breathless owner.

Michael Jones

The Airedale Therapist

The 'Dales are befuddled, bewildered and cuddly when anyone here is sick.

1. "Hey-where's our breakfast? Dontcha know it's 6 AM and we have to go out?"
2. "How come you're making all that noise in the bathroom-we better check you over, just in case." {BIGNOSEPOKES}
3. "Whatryadoin back in bed?-dontcha wanna play (BIGNOSEPOKES)?"
4. "Here, lean on me if you're feeling tippy over."
5. "Guess we better guard our Hooman and lie down by the bed 'till this is over."

Yvonne Michalak

Misty is my nurse. Once I managed to get a really bad case of pee-you-monia. It was so bad that my doctor threatened to put me in hospital. I begged him not to, as we live 20 miles outside of town and my husband is legally blind and does not drive. I promised the Doctor I would go home and get in bed and stay there. Home I came. Misty took one sniff and followed me to the bedroom. She lay down beside me with her head on my pillow beside me until I was just about asleep and then moved herself to the side of the bed where I would have to step out if I were to get up. Every time I attempted to get out of bed for the next 24 hours, she growled at me. Frankly I think the doctor bribed her.

Right now I am suffering from a very severe knee problem. I cannot manage (as yet) to go from a seated position to a standing one unless I am on the couch. Every time I crawl to the couch she growls at me (tail wagging) and tries to help by getting in front of me and licking my face.

D'Arlene-Anne Kapenga

Toby had her first training session for hearing assistance work today. First thing Richard the trainer said when he arrived for the evaluation was, "I see you've kept the weight off her." A working dog has to be fit. Today I asked Richard what he was looking for when he evaluated Toby. He mentioned several things: orality (a willingness to poke and prod with the mouth and nose), energy level (pretty high, but not hyperactive), owner's control and basic obedience skills, attention level, alertness. More terriers should be assistance dogs!

We are starting off with three tasks-two way seek (I tell Toby to seek Ansley and Toby brings Ansley to me, and vice versa), bringing me to the door when someone is there, and telling me when people/ bikes/cars are coming up behind me. This will probably take 15-18 weeks. Today we started the two-way seek. Toby had a lot of fun. I think she is really suited for this.

Jessica Rabin

Soon after receiving a phone call notifying my family of the unexpected death of my brother-in-law, I sat heavily down on the living room sofa softly crying. Just then, Airedale Duke quietly approached me and dropped his favorite toy, a plastic Snoopy dog, in my lap. I could not help but laugh and began to feel better immediately.

Terry Wertan

A few months ago my dad was hospitalized because of a heart attack and due to complications, he was gone for about 10 days. Over the two years that we have Max, personal items of my dad's regularly went missing, some without explanation and some hidden behind the couch in our family room, which happens to be Max's place. When my dad arrived home after his stay in the hospital, no one was happier to see him than Max-he had missed him so much. For the 10 days my dad was gone Max was sad, listless, not eating well, had low energy; in a word, he was heartbroken. When my dad returned, one by one the missing items would appear outside his bedroom door-an old slipper, a baseball hat, an eyeglass case, an old newspaper. Every item made my father laugh; he says it was his best medicine.

Denise Cuevas

My mother-in-law had a very difficult life. Her husband died when she was pretty young, leaving her with a small child and no means of support. She worked and studied for her degree, then worked 2 jobs almost her whole life. She forgot how to laugh. It was really very sad; in 15 years of my marriage I had never seen her laugh.

She did not like dogs and was against our idea of getting a puppy. I think Max was about 6-7 months old when this happened: I came home from work to find my mother-in-law laughing loudly and with such a pleasure! It turned out she was watching Max working out the way to open one of the kitchen cabinets. She loves Max, as we all do, and it's much easier for her to laugh now.

Margarita Revzin

One of the most amazing and puzzling things that the Lovely Rita ever did happened on the first day of school, as my prior marriage to PF was failing. I had had some minor surgery, after which my husband had left to work out of town for a week. He returned, and was going to be home for the first week of school. I was not pleased, for those first few days of school are invariably harried, disorganized, and stressful enough to drive a saint to swear.

When I returned home at the end of that first long, tiring day, PF's car there in the driveway to further annoy me, I discovered that the Lovely Rita had been thinking of me that day. The door to my office was open just a crack, and right there in the corner lay an arrangement left for me by Rita.

The "Arrangement" included a terra cotta potsherd that Rita had treasured since she was a very small puppy. All of the rough edges had been filed down by her puppy teeth; I had no fear that she would splinter it, as she took VERY good care of this treasure. There was also a grape, split but not eaten, that I had given her that morning to play with. A lone piece of grass rounded out the composition. It resembled Indian sign...or maybe voodoo....or perhaps it was even a canine form of poetry.

What I have no doubt of is that it was deliberate, and it was done for ME.

Gena Welch

My mom is in the hospital having broken her leg-the same leg-for the second time since mid-November. While visiting I asked the staff if I could bring a dog to visit her. They said "Only if the dog bites." I explained that would rule out all seven of my gang. They said that in lieu of biting, they would accept a dog who was current on his/her shots. (A very funny group, as you can see.) Well yesterday, Henry my Honey had his face all combed and we proceeded to visit the hospital. He was his usual big woolly cuddle-bug self and had staff coming out of the walls to visit him. Several people had stories of past Airedales in their families. Of course, Mom was delighted to have the woolly boy there and it didn't hurt that they were giving her lunch at the time of our visit-she had Henry's complete and total attention. I am sure pleased to be able to tell everyone that this sweet boy was rescued from our local kill facility and that he routinely puts smiles on the faces of nursing home residents.

Cheryl Silver

Many of the people we visit in hospitals and nursing homes readily recognize an Airedale, due in part to the fact that when these people were younger, that was a time when Airedales were at their peak of popularity. Don't forget, these people lived through one and, in many cases, two World Wars and we all know Airedales were used a lot in various capacities during the WW's, (messengers, sentry, Red Cross) hence Airedales appeared on magazine covers, post cards, etc. We find the dogs that prompt the most discussion are the Irish Wolfhound and Newfoundland because of their size ("How much do they eat?" and "Boy, they're big!") and the Airedales for the memories they rekindle. Many people have fondly recalled the Airedales they had, or knew of, when they were young.

I remember one man in particular telling me about the Airedale he had had as a child, how it would pull him on a sled and would wait at the end of his driveway watching for him when he walked home from school. He laughed as he told me it was "the most stubborn dawg" he ever knew. Then, as his withered hand gently stroked my Airedale's head, he added, "But he was my best friend. Boy, I sure loved that dawg."

Shelley DeMerchant

CHAPTER FIVE

Antics

ADT owners, to the uneducated eye, can seem as odd as their dogs in the antics they find funny-mayhem, destruction, injury. They actively encourage their animals up on the furniture and will talk the ear off anyone who shows even the remotest interest in Airedales.

It took all of us a while to figure out what was happening during our New Year's eve sit down gourmet feast: our napkins kept disappearing. As hostess, I recall, subconsciously, noting several guests doing what people do when they can't locate the napkin they had placed on their laps. Zoe (just over a year) had quietly, without touching anyone, slipped the napkins from the laps, disappeared with them around the corner and destroyed them with gusto. I still don't know how her woolly head and JAWSOFDEATH escaped detection for as long as they did. Of course, being the darling of the guests, she was allowed to continue unobstructed, but watched with amused delight, until everyone was sans napkin (or in Canadianese, sans serviette).

Anne Clarke

Yesterday, we went to the humane society for pictures with Santa Paws, as a fund raiser. Ahead of us were all single dogs or small duos (quite cute in their biker leather outfits). As Santa Paws eyes my fuzzy duo, he asks will they get up on the couch LOL. Hope jumps up first on her side, Angus jumps up on the opposite. As Santa tries to scooch between them, Angus stares directly into his face and his eyes register the fact that this person has a fuzzy face. (Remember this is the dog that didn't recognize his mom when she applied a green facial until I spoke). He was beside himself with joy that a human could have a beard (and it was real). Santa was most patient as Angus explored and tentatively pulled.

I really hope I don't know what he asked for for Christmas; I'll be carefully checking my chin in the mirror for a while.

Gale H. Ford

This morning started off with my macaw doing his usual morning talk/scream session. Somewhere in the middle of this he got himself pretty worked up and moved into his all out, completely obnoxious, bloody murder yell that is normally reserved for times when an unknown individual approaches the house. Dallin hopped up on "her" cedar chest in front of the livingroom window to see who was there. After a quick look told her that we really didn't have company, she ran to the birds' room, looked at the macaw and gave one bark which, combined with the disgusted look on her face very definitely said, "Shut up bird!"

Trish Ganter

My sister's Airedale Andi (big, woolly, smart) was Queen of the Neighborhood. One of the ways she exercised her office was Noise Control. When all the neighborhood dogs began barking their fool heads off, Andi would mince her way over to the end of her run, draw herself up tall and stiff, and say ONCE, firmly but not too loudly "BFFFT!!!" and they would all immediately shut up. When I tell that story people do not believe me-unless they have ever known an Airedale.

Gena Welch

Yet another testimony to how smart Airedales are-and how gullible their owners can be. Last night, Toby and I were sitting on the sofa. I was drinking a beer and reading, and she was "resting" (I now realize she was plotting).

Toby looks alert, runs to the sliding glass door and barks. I leave my beer on the end table and go to the door to see what's happening.

Nothing. I turn around, and there's Toby, licking the mouth of my beer can. It can be challenging living with a rocket scientist dog.

Jessica Rabin

This past week Kelsey (just over a year) learned a new skill. Since Trotter, our ten year old rescue, came to live with us, Kelsey felt that she wasn't getting enough attention. She tried flirting, teasing, being a nuisance, anything to keep Trotter from getting his share of attention.

A few days ago she finally solved the problem. When Trotter goes into the laundry room to eat, Kelsey gets behind the door, pushes it closed, and then leans on it to make it latch. Poor Trotter must wonder why he is in the dark so often.

We tried a door stop but Kelsey just pushed harder and made more noise. This afternoon she closed and latched the door on my husband and Trotter. I've never had a dog that was such a problem-solver. She makes things happen-and it scares me. What might be next?

Gretchen Kish

My Sugar (Lave's Precious Golddust UD) had never gone down on a sit-stay, so I felt confident after what I thought was a very nice job in Open B. The week before this show, the same grounds had housed the county fair and the building was full of flies. When I returned on the sit-stay, there was my "never did it," nice working Airedale lying down! Well, that was bad enough; but when the judge finished handing out awards, she leaned over the gate and said, "Your dog is the finest fly catcher I ever saw but it cost her first place with a 197 1/2." Still, Sugar was top dog over all breeds in Wisconsin two years in a row and top Airedale in Terriers for the same two years.

LaVerne Van Der Zee

I worry about the people who come into my sign shop and see Maggie behind the counter. They all think that they want an Airedale based on her behavior at work. She is so calm and ignores most of the people who come in. I sure don't want them to get the idea that Airedales just lie around and sleep all the time. I have made a sign which is on the front counter that tells the true story about Maggie, all her surgery because of hip dysplasia and how different she acts once she gets home. They all read the sign and look at me as if I am not telling the truth.

Carolyn Finlayson

Today Keeper entered full-scale Airedalehood. Her ceremony was so well timed, so simple yet effective that I can only compare it to a Bat Mitzvah. Background: a warm, sunny day (finally). I decided to wear a dress, nothing fancy and OK for dog slobber because I was taking Keeper to the vet in the afternoon and didn't want to change. It would be nice to present myself at the clinic in a clean and neat state for once, instead of in the usual unwashed and sweatclothes style in which I usually arrive. The hours passed in happy (ha) work.

A little while before Keeper and I were due to leave, I let all the dogs out. Brought them in ten minutes before it was time to leave. Keeper was prancing happily and grinning. Keeper reeked of engine grease. She had rolled in the spot where, it turned out, Farmer John had been repairing the Rototiller last night, allowing thick, filthy, stinky, engine grease to drip on the grass. Keeper was slicked with grease on her ear, leg, side, and back.

The ADT hooman is quick of thought and action. Pausing only to strangle John (or I would have except that he's more than a foot taller than I), I shut the dogs in the laundry room, ran upstairs and exchanged my dress for slob shorts and tee. Gathering towels, two kinds of dog shampoo, and treats, I ran and got Keeper. Ran her upstairs and into the tub. Scrub, scrub, scrub, fastest bath in the West. Washed and rinsed her twice, towelled her, ran her down to the car and off we went to the vet's, arriving on time and in our usual state with her somewhat clean and me a filthy mess.

She was there for her rabies shot and stomach x-ray to check if the plastic lion she had eaten had passed through her system or was still stuck. The vet greeted her with a jaunty pat on the butt and she cringed away, so he fed her treats during her entire visit. I said, "I think she's faking it by now," and he agreed that she understood that if she looked afraid, he'd give her a treat. To complete my happiness, we discovered the errant piece of plastic she ate in Feb. is still lodged in Keeper's stomach. This indicates it's too big to go through the bowels; if it does, it's likely to cause a blockage. Further consultations are in order, since we're looking at surgery.

Here is a useful piece of information: the vet said to wash her in Dawn dish detergent; it's the soap of choice for oil spills. I did that this evening but still haven't removed all the grease. Montana Barbara suggested using peanut butter to get the remaining grease off Keeper. It really works. Here's what you do: grab a big jar of smooth peanut butter and run upstairs to the torture chamber (bathroom). Seeing the jar, the dogs will follow. Get the non-bathers out of the room by putting a dab of peanut butter (PB) behind their top front teeth and shove them out the door while they're licking. Spread big dabs of PB on the far side of the tub so the bather jumps into the tub and starts licking it away. Quickly saturate the grease-covered areas of the dog with water and wash with Dawn or a citrus-based grease dissolver. Rinse rinse rinse and use a skin-soothing creme rinse if you have one. You can rinse the whole dog but don't wash the whole dog. After drying the dog, you can slap on some oatmeal or tea tree skin soother.

Sherry Rind

After help from Merlin and Sarah this morning, I was about 45 minutes late for work. We recycle newspapers and plastics and have two large Rubbermaid tubs for holding until Cathy or I take them to the recycling center-one for newspapers and one for the various plastics. Now on the top 10 list of favorite things which go SNAP-CRACKLE-POP when the ADT chews them must be the empty 2-liter plastic bottle, and there HAD BEEN about 50 or 60 of them in the plastics tub last night. However, before leaving for work this morning I let Merlin and Sarah out to go potty one last time and then the phone rang.

When I went out to call them, I noticed a trail of plastic grocery bags heading from the garage to the back yard. Then I noticed an EMPTY recycling tub. Well, almost empty-it had exactly ONE 2-liter bottle left in it. Oh, wait-there came Sarah running at top speed to me, nooooo, past me. Diving into the tub, she deftly retrieved the last bottle and took off past me with it in the JAWSOFDEATH (crackling nicely, I might add) and darted into the back yard. When I went out into the yard, I saw the ADT recycling project. Neatly dispersed over the entire back yard were about 50 or 60 plastic bottles in random locations everywhere. Under the swingset. Under the deck. On the grass. In the ivy. Everywhere. Even at the edge of the grass-clipping dumping area which is so close to the invisible fence wire that I couldn't figure out how they got it there until I saw both of them take bottles and throw them and then run after them. They were having an absolutely wonderful time with all those bottles. It only took about 45 minutes for mean old daddy to pick up all the new toys, put them back in their tub, and incarcerate the re-cyclists back in the house for the day.

Bill Austin

I am a craftsman, a woodworker who specializes in boat carpentry. For 13 years my constant work companion was a gentle, mild mannered English springer spaniel named Cutter. My wife had an Airedale in the late 60's and I liked what I knew of them but had never known one on an intimate basis. Nothing I had read and nothing she said prepared me for my first Airedale puppy! I knew that they were referred to as a thinking dog, but what I didn't read until much later is that they have a penchant for being willfully disobedient. They never forget anything. They just ignore the command when it isn't in their plan or if you don't have a bribe waiting in your hand.

When Chester took over our lives, he was four months old. We didn't know what was happening, only that he was cute and really needed a playmate. Two months later we drove back (22 hours round-trip!) to get his sister, Hanna. Now we have two terrorists with which we share our home. I now know that the Airedale's preference for paper as a major source of fiber in their diet is almost universal in the breed. During the puppy phase of my training, they ate rolls of masking tape, duct tape, wood tape and chewed up a fortune in sandpaper. Nothing was, or is (three years later) safe. There were the usual problems of keeping them out of the bathrooms so that they wouldn't eat the tissue paper from the trash can or the convenient self- feeding pop-up box.

Chester took control of the shop, raiding the workbenches for anything they could consume. I carried (notice the past tense) my tools in those LL Bean canvas bags, heavy-duty canvas with extra thick handles. He bit all the handles in two-he didn't chew them; he would just walk up to them and bite the handle in half. I now had several bags with four straight tabs where two handles had existed before. He pulled the same trick with leashes; the cut ends wouldn't even be wet, just a clean cut all the way through. He would still be by my side, just no longer on lead.

Hanna decided her favorite hunting grounds would be my office with its endless supply of papers resting on the desk and in the trash basket. Post-it notes, bills, letters, junk mail and her personal favorite-PAPER MONEY-could no longer be left unguarded. The good news is that we almost always retrieved the money (gives new meaning to money laundering), the office is less cluttered and she hasn't figured out how to operate that new expensive trash can with the step-on pop-top lid.

The woodworking shop was the biggest problem as there were always new projects underway with a steady stream of supplies arriving on the loading dock. It's still not uncommon to find a neat little pile of screws out in the back yard with their cardboard container missing in action. I'm not always as prompt as I should be in making sure that the shop is safe for the dogs or that the shop is safe from the dogs.

In the rush to finish my work and get to the job site one day, I accepted a shipment from the UPS-a cardboard shipping box of 25 sq. ft. of teak parquet flooring and a can of adhesive-set it on the floor of the shop, and forgot about it. The next time I looked at it, there was no box, just a perfectly neat stack of flooring with the can of adhesive sitting on top. They had eaten the entire box. There was not a shred of cardboard or packing paper on the floor. Nothing, not a trace of evidence anywhere except for those Airedale grins.

Michael Jones & Judith Powers

My delightfully devilish Daisy has been an ear-licker par excellence since day one. I remember walking her in the park one day and some boys were rolling down a hill like logs. Daisy was entranced and kept trying to scamper along with them to get at their ears as they rolled by.

There is a set of twin boys down the street who learned years ago of Daisy's fetish and would come and sit on the curb when they saw her coming so she could do her "duty" on their ears. If she missed one, they would point it out to her and she would finish the job. (Now they are teenagers and wouldn't do this for the world.)

Capitalizing on Mike Tyson's shameful biting of Evander Holyfield's (sp?) ear, my friend Frank would, to the amusement of all present, point to his ear while leaning close to Daisy, and say "Tyson, Tyson" and Daisy would oblige by going for the ear. Silly, silly, silly.

Cheryl Silver

Whilst Kimbee and I were in California, Ranger was busy pickin' the locks on his brand-spankin' new crate twice, and meeting the pet-sitter at the door-this was after pulling nearby rugs INTO the crate! How the heck he got a two-foot by six-foot hallway runner into the crate is beyond Copperfield, all this while sliding the floor pan out.

'Dale Burrier

Half a year ago I wouldn't dream of combining Dina with royalty. But now she is beginning to show a superior attitude to dogs and humans that is very royal. The latest example: Some days ago I heard the "Come-and-help-me" bark upstairs. I went up, and saw Dina staring at her bed. In the middle there was a tennis ball. I removed the ball; she went into bed and gave me a friendly upper-class look saying: "Thank you, James, that will be all for now. You may go."

Kjell Sjostrom

Our housekeeper, who cleans weekly, insists on wearing skirts with a kick-pleat (a slit) in the back. Madie's favorite weekly nosepoke is from the rear, through the slit and upward resulting in a shriek and jump. Since the housekeeper is about 180 lbs. she does not get great elevation, but the shriek is quite noteworthy.

Dorothy Dunn Duff

Our fifteen year old daughter found herself a "Nosepoke Hall of Fame" entry yesterday. Mr. Woofer, who stands about 30" at the shoulder (that's about 34" at nosepoke height), came up behind Shani (26" inseam on her jeans, counting the 2" that drapes over her shoes and drags on the ground). His El Penultimo Nosepoke included a LIFT which resulted in a full TWO FEET of daylight between Shani's butt and Mr. Woofer's head at the zenith. Her ensuing shriek shattered windows and glassware for miles around.

Subtracting the 2" of inseam that drags on the ground, then adding the resulting 24" to the 24" of daylight revealed by the Nosepoke, I calculate Mr. Woofer's nosepoke to be an even four feet of elevation. Any challengers?

Chuck Shaddoway

Over on this side of the pond we tend to concentrate on style, subtlety and inventiveness rather than mere height. Although still a relative novice, Ruaridh has had some staggering successes. Picture a well-endowed lady in tight floral pants bending over to lift shopping out of her car. Before I can shout "Leave it!" a quick

NOSEPOKE catapults the lady into the back of the car, sprawling among her groceries. Fortunately, she found this funny but unfortunately gave Ruaridh a biscuit, thereby making sure he'll repeat this behaviour.

The NOSEPOKES at the Highland Games, I will leave to your imagination but suffice it to say that records were broken in the caber tossing that day!

Cherry Welsh, Scotland

As I was thinking about Nell lifting up my bathrobe in the back (and the back yard!) it occurred to me how similar this breed is across cultures. Whether the dog lives in Australia, the US, Canada, Scotland, France, Denmark, Japan, South Africa, Malaysia or any other country, when one of us describes the conduct or moves of our ADTs, all the other listers understand. And they've usually experienced it themselves. I could visit any of you in other countries and see something that would make me feel right at home-the NOSEPOKE, the WETBEARDKISS. Airedale culture is world wide.

Mary Giese

I was standing at the bathroom sink cleaning my contact lenses, Keeper sitting beside me, when Darwin came trotting in with that special neck-arched prance that means he was carrying something in his mouth. I assumed he had a toy and wanted Keeper to chase him, so I teasingly said, "Oh, what's Darwin got?" Just as it finally dawned on me that he might be carrying something that he shouldn't have, he went downstairs. I grabbed some treats that I had cleverly left on the bathroom counter and trotted to the top of the stairs to call him back. He looked but wouldn't come until he saw me giving Keeper a treat.

When he came upstairs, I easily took the object from his mouth and gave him a treat. He had had the object inside his mouth without gripping it in his teeth. It was a small candy bar, wet and slimy but without a dent in it. I remembered I'd left it in the tote bag I'd been carrying all day with files and other work. All evening that tote bag had lain in my study, untouched on the floor beside my desk, while I'd been in and out of there working. Earlier I had thought Darwin was being unusually affectionate, lying close by my feet while I worked, because I'd been gone all day. I should have known he was guarding his treat and biding his time! I'm so proud of him: he's showing signs of getting smarter and smarter.

Sherry Rind

When Calamity hurt her foot a while back, the treatment was soaking twice a day. What worked best for us was to use a tall, narrow plastic drinking glass or similarly-shaped Rubbermaid container-the opening was only about three inches across-and just a small amount of soaking solution. I sat on the floor with Calamity wedged into a corner so she couldn't run away. Then I put her paw all the way into the container so that she could not bend her "wrist," and I held her "elbow" straight. The result was that her right leg was pretty much immobilized. Now you can't do this for an hour or something, but I could keep everything in place for five or ten minutes at a time. Because the soaking solution was in a tall, narrow container, there wasn't any splashing and a relatively small amount to clean up on the couple of occasions that she managed to break loose.

A funny aspect of that injury. The vet recommended soaking in an acidic solution and suggested that an inexpensive, easily-available choice was "feminine hygiene solution." So I, being the good father that I am, dropped the dog at home and went to Target and picked up two economy-size boxes of douche and headed for the checkout line. As the attractive young female cashier rang up my purchases, she gave me quite a strange look. I didn't know whether to let her think whatever she wanted, or tell her that it was for my dog. I figured it was a no-win situation and kept quiet. And I swear, when I returned several days later for more, I got the same cashier!

Jim Mattimoe

It happens in the middle of the night. We're all asleep, including Murphy. It starts out real soft, then gets louder and louder. It's sort of a wooo, but more of a hoooooo. I heard this for the first time in 1972 at an ATCGP club meeting at Birchrun Kennels. Adele and Barbara had four ADTs upstairs and a whole raft of them in the kennels in the basement. Our meeting was progressing nicely and one dog somewhere started the AAAWWWOOOOOOOO and all the rest picked up on it. STEREO! It makes the hair on the back of your neck stand up! We nicknamed it the Birchrun Chorus.

Mine occasionally do it and almost always in the wee hours. The funniest instance of this was when we tried to take a vacation back in the early '80's. We boarded all 5 ADTs with a poodle friend who has a small kennel. The kennel is in a wooded area about 100 feet from the house. On the first night my dogs were there, the owners reported they heard a strange sound almost like wind in the trees. They went outside and determined it was coming from the kennel. They sneaked in and looked (night light was on) and there were the 5 ADTs sitting by the gates of their runs, all looking straight ahead and sending forth the moaning sound. One of the owners made a noise and it immediately stopped and didn't recur for the 5 nights they were there. The owners had never in all their years with dogs ever heard such a sound from any other breed.

Jack McLaughlin

Mr. Chuggy, my 2 year old foster wild child, and I had a very good weekend until Sunday evening. He learned "down" and actually got me up to go outside to go potty. Our early morning snuggle sessions are becoming habit and he makes me laugh at the strangest things. He ran out of the room when I sneezed, only to peer around the corner at me to see if things were okay. I guess when you've spent your whole life tied up outside, sneezes would be new noises.

Anyway, I bend over to kiss the top of his lovely head and he decides to leap up to meet me. My face meets the bowling ball head and a fat lip is the result. The rest of the evening is uneventful. This morning the fat lip is now a lovely shade of purple. While I'm iron-ing my clothes for work, I hear a strange crunching sound. I'm sure like many of you, I've become quite adept at determining what differ-ent objects sound like when they are being chewed on, but this is a new one. Upon investigation I find he is chewing my glasses! I've had these glasses for 3 years, so am kind of unsure where any of my old pairs would be, so I head upstairs to rooms that are normally closed off to look for them. Chuggy of course, comes along. This is new ter-ritory for him, he's never been in these rooms before. As I'm going through a dresser drawer looking for the glasses, I look over and guess who is leaving his "mark" on the wall? By the time I get stuff cleaned up, it's time for me to go to work. As I need my glasses to function, I just wear my sunglasses. So into work I go-I'm a case-worker at the local Social Services office-with a bruised upper lip, wearing my sunglasses. At least only 2 people asked if I had been beaten up! And to think, I'm still thinking about adopting this lug!

Linda L. Cunningham

Kugel & I are located in the suburbs of Boston. I challenge the authorities sometimes. Most cases, it is not a big deal. People recog-nize Kugel's obedient and non-aggressive personality and dismiss the rules altogether. I think they are for the leashless and angry-dog types. And, I only take her to generic places like the hardware store, the library, post office, floral shoppe, gym, gas station. But on the rare occasion when I am challenged; I look the person right in the eye when they point at the "No Dogs Allowed" sign and I reply: "This is not a dog, this is an AIREDALE." It's always amazing when the per-son backs down and replies, "Oh? O.K."

Kiwi Karley

I admit I consider Fiona a member of the family. But I don't normally expect other people to see her that way. So imagine my panic and then surprise and relief as the following conversation un-folds. This morning I'm on the phone with my mother back East. She has been out to Oregon and met Fiona once. My mother mentions that she has Christmas presents for all nine grandkids. I immediately go into a panic, wheels turning in my head. Nine? Nine?? I had only eight on my list! Was I in the Bad Aunt Corner again? How old was number nine? Had I missed a birthday? Had one of my brothers recently acquired another offspring and had I failed to notice? My mother continued to enumerate her gift list, as I gave her half an ear, trying to count heads. (My sister's four, my eldest brother's one. Who was I missing?) My mother concluded, "And I got Fiona the cutest stuffed toys-a banana and a hot dog." Phew! I was off the hook! And mind you, none of my siblings' dogs or cats was on the list.

Mary Heinricher

It's 4.30 pm on Christmas Day in Palmerston North New Zealand and my ADTs are all 3 fast asleep on the couches after a Christmas treat. I've had a great day and it is so hot and sunny. Sorry for you folks in the Northern hemisphere; I hear that you got cold weather. Wish I could send you some sun. Tui, Gracie and Becky Ru have all had a great Christmas day. I went out for dinner and came back to find Tui's paws and mouth covered in blood and to my relief she had only killed a rodent and eaten it as she thinks I don't feed her enough.

Sue Martin

Airedales sure know how to get one's attention! Dallin asked to go out in the middle of the night so I obediently got up and let her out. A few hours later, and still before I wanted to get up, she was back with that cold nose of hers, poke poke poke. I rolled over and asked her if she really really had to go. She walked away and I thought I was safe to doze off again. A minute later I heard the sound of her drinking water. Seconds after that she was back setting that wet beard on my bare arm. If the cold nose won't do, how about a wet beard for you? I got up and let her out.

Trish Ganter

I have 3 Airedales who are thrilled over the freezing cold. This morning I was watching them out the window and it was so touching. All 3 were playing together. Then Nell and Toggle started horsing around and Charlie felt left out. So he went after Toggle, shoving him and growling. Nell immediately got into the middle and calmed Charlie down. Seconds later they were all playing again.

A bit later Charlie got ruffled again. Next thing I know, Nell is on one side licking Charlie's ears, which he loves, and Toggle was on the other side doing the same thing. Then they all joined in to play again. It is wonderful to see how they resolve these conflicts. Then they all came in and had hot chocolate made with carob powder and milk with a bit of acidophilus in it to avoid upset stomachs. Now they are all napping so I can get some work done.

Mary Giese

A few years back, we traveled to Victoria, BC and panicked at the last minute when we discovered we didn't have Bonnie's rabies certificate with us, much less any other shot records. After a round of "Why didn't you check this out?" and "You can dial the phone too?" between family members, we decided to disguise Bonnie ADT as one of the boys. My son Scott put his baseball cap on her head and she sat in the seat between them just like she was one of the kids. I took a picture of her sitting there with a big smile on her face.

She has no doubt she's the most important kid of all. Just ask either of my sons, they'll say Bonnie is the most spoiled child in the family. Up until Beau came along anyway. Back to the reason for the email-no one asked for rabies certificates either coming or going. I don't know if we were just lucky or Bonnie's disguise was very convincing.

Judy Dwiggins

Yesterday, it was so nice here, that I took Otis and Milo for a ride to the ocean. It is a few hours away. All went well, Otis and Milo ran on the beach for approximately 7 miles, chased seagulls, and basically had a blast. On the way home they were both sound asleep. I was driving, and was going 44 in a 30. I really thought it was 40 mph road, but bottom line is: they got me!

I pulled over, and Otis and Milo woke up to all the bright lights. They went straight for the driver's window to see what was going on. I did not hold them back, just in case I did not like this cop, either. Next, as the lady officer was walking up to the van, I heard her repeating, "It's OK, guys. It's OK." She was very friendly, and they sort of liked her. Come to find out she used to have an Airedale. I told her I was just coming home from taking them to the beach. She thought that was so nice of me! I never did find my registration, but while I was looking she was having a conversation with O & M about the beach. She checked my license, and then proceeded to talk about Airedales.

So here we are at 10 PM on the side of the road with all the lights going, talking Airedales. We talked and talked. People that lived nearby must have been wondering when the paddy wagon was going to come to take me away, as we were there so long! In the end, she apologized for waking them up, both dogs got a kiss, and she told me to have a nice night! No ticket, no warning and this time I can THANK DOG! I guess they earned many extra treats for that one. After all, they could have snarled at her; instead they just charmed her to death. And because of TFAOP we all went away smiling!

Shirley Sanborn

CHAPTER SIX

Puppies: The Inside and Outside Scoop

PEOPLE WHO HAVE RAISED an Airedale puppy will recognize many of the stories that follow because you have lived them. You will also find useful information on what to look for in a puppy and, equally important, in the breeder. As in the training chapter, you will also find solutions not covered in your usual training manual because the Airedale is not your usual dog.

The ADT puppy stage lasts for up to three years with some harrowing experiences during that time. Amazingly, they and their owners generally come through in fine form, with the owners starting to yearn for another puppy and even travelling to visit breeders just to inhale that intoxicating puppy smell.

Whelping

One evening after we arrived home from a party, our bitch wanted out into the large enclosure. We expected her puppies soon but thought it would be OK to let her out for a moment. About 5 minutes later we heard the unmistakable noises of puppy squeaks coming from under the concrete stairs attached to the house. We had to dig with shovels for 20 minutes to get the bitch and 4 or 5 puppies out from under the steps. A watched Airedale will not whelp but put them under the stairs in an awkward situation and they will have puppies in a second.

We were covered in dirt from head to foot and it was raining. The puppies were all OK and all was well, but we never again let bitches who are close out in the large pen. She had a beautiful whelping box in the basement and a heat lamp and clean papers, etc.; but, oh no, she chose dirt and cold and privacy under the steps. You could bury a Volkswagen in the hole she dug in 5 minutes.

Joanne B. Helm

I was lucky to be well mentored the one time we had puppies. On the expected eve, I moved Roxy to the utility/computer/civil defense radio lounge and had the plastic swimming pool all fixed up with nice comfy blankies. And I slept on the floor with her that night. Good thing because she went into labor at 6 AM and started popping out puppies. At 7 she stopped. After a half hour or so, she seemed a little bewildered and miserable so I let her outside figuring she'd come right back in to the puppies after she piddled. SHE DISAPPEARED IN THE FENCED YARD. I panicked and called my Airedale buddy who rushed up to help look.

She was in a den under the greenhouse. Humongous den. Held 3 adult 'dales later in the summer. Digging would not get her out but fortunately she was willing to come out for baloney. She then delivered 3 more pups.

"Alaska Carol" Dickinson

When Misty had her litter, I had never been anywhere near a whelping dog, so I was going by the book. That night she panted a lot, so I really wanted her to stay in the whelping box that Randy had so painstakingly made for her. She wanted to be with Dad in bed, so I ended up sleeping on the floor by the box with her inside. Oh, was I sore and tired the next morning and in a panic. I could not figure out how to get Misty to push (now don't laugh; it isn't nice). I called the vet; I was sure she was in labor. He calmed me down and told me that a dog's system kind of pushes itself and I didn't have to tell her to push and then to breathe (all those birthing class tapes for nothing).

I was so wiped out that I did something I usually don't do. I stayed home from work, slept all day until in the late evening Randy came in to wake me and tell me Misty's water had broken or something (can't remember what, but we knew it was a go). I got her in the whelping box and sat with her. Then the first one came: ohhhhh, soooo cute. Couldn't keep my hands off it-had to help. The next one came and Misty looked at me like, "Well, you gonna do this one, too?" at which point Randy threatened to tie my hands to my sides if I did anything more than pull the membrane away from their mouths. It only took about three hours. She did a beautiful job. She and I put little rick rack around them to tell them apart and made a chart to weigh them every other day and I tried to be there when she nursed as often as I could-kind of a mother-daughter thing.

D'Arlene-Anne Kapenga

Buying a Puppy

When interviewing prospective owners, I cover a lot of the topics included in my puppy package as well as the contract and I give them a list of suggested books to obtain. At that time I also show the owners copies of the parent's hip clearance certificates and litter registration form. (In Canada, unlike in the US according to law, it is the responsibility of the seller to provide Canadian Kennel Club registration papers to the new owners and the seller is responsible for the registration and transfer costs.)

I used to send the puppy information packages along with the pups. However, I was finding that, with the excitement of a new puppy in the home, the owners didn't get an opportunity to really sit down and thoroughly read over a puppy package. So now I either give them the puppy package when they make their pick or courier it to them the week before they pick up their puppy.

The puppy package contains a covering letter and detailed information on: history of the Airedale Terrier, bringing puppy home, first days in the new home, house training, crate training, size/type of crate to get, training tips, importance of obedience training, feeding schedule, recommended food (if the brand I feed is not available in their area), how to switch over food/water, veterinary care, vaccination schedule, what to discuss with vet, teething, chewing, nail clipping, ear cleaning, tips on getting advice, hospital etiquette, common sense stuff on how to avoid communicable diseases (especially parvo), poisonous plants, grooming, naming your puppy (hints on picking a call name and requirements for registered name), puppy proofing your home, suggested books, explanation of tattoo numbers, what to do/who to contact if their dog is lost or stolen, bio on parents and bio on us. I include photos of the litter, their pup and their pup's parents; pamphlets and brochures about different kinds of heartworm/flea preventions; lyme disease; spaying/neutering, etc. There is also a five generation pedigree, several of our business cards, my vet's business card, and an application for membership in the Airedale Terrier Club of Canada.

A couple of weeks before the pups go (usually when owners do their "pick") I have the new owners bring me a "receiving blanket." When they pick up their pup, they take their own receiving blanket back with them, hence it has the familiar scent of my home and the littermates on it. The day they pick up their puppy, they also receive: a health record; a copy of the completed, signed & witnessed contract (denoting tattoo # and CKC litter registration #); a copy of the completed, signed & witnessed non-breeding agreement; the bill of sale, a new leash and collar, chew toy, 18 LB bag of food and large jug(s) of water.

I also follow up with a phone call the next morning to make sure the night went well and another phone call a couple of days later. For the first few months (to help new owners over the teething/house training stage) I'm in regular contact with the owners and always available to answer questions. I expect and receive photos of the puppies in their new homes and we keep a photo album on each litter. We also host an Airedale Puppy Reunion Party at our home every year and each puppy gets a phone call on its "special day" to wish them a Happeee Burfday! Am I fanatical? You betcha and proud of it! I really like the idea of including a copy of this book and possibly Dorothy Miner's book.

Shelley DeMerchant

Bob and I had both had puppies before, of different breeds, so we thought we knew what to expect. When we arrived at the Airedale house, we were attacked by eight black and tan tornadoes. Never had I seen anything like it. I almost left. I was sure there wouldn't be any shoes or socks left on my feet when the dust cleared. Heavens, I wasn't sure there'd be any feet.

Bob decided one was calmer than the others. How he came to that decision, I have no clue; however, after an hour and several Band-Aids, we left with the dream puppy. I had a nice box in the back seat and I sat with her so that she wouldn't be scared. Dog was bored to death. The only time she responded to me was to waddle over to my side ("Oh, my puppy wants to say hello," says the fool) and throw up in my lap. Heaven forbid she should get her box dirty. She then returned to the middle of the box to sleep. Gave me one final look that said, "Now will you shut up!" The queen got out several times on the three-hour drive home to pee and chase bugs; she threw up a couple more times, always aiming for me. She was totally unconcerned about leaving Mom and her litter mates. Tegan never whined, ever.

We had a large crate at home for her, Great Dane size. When we got home, I put her in the crate to rest. Actually, I was the one who needed rest. She sat in the crate, right behind the door. She looked at us. She looked at the door to the crate. She never turned around to inspect the rest of the crate, just the door. She then looked at us again, hard. We made stupid puppy noises. She then proceeded to throw a hissy fit. There is really no other way to describe it. Never have I seen an animal do this before. Kids, yes, but not dogs.

She tried to rip the door off the hinges. Broke a tooth, blood everywhere. In pain? No, madder than h*ll. Bob and I just looked at each other, dumbfounded. "The dog is insane!" was our first thought. Finally, after about five minutes, she stopped, stomped to the back of the kennel and threw herself on the floor. If looks could kill, Bob and I would have been ashes.

After about half an hour, I opened the door to let her out, now that she had been quiet. I called her. One eye opened. I made stupid puppy noises trying to get her to come to me. She let me make stupid puppy noises. She lay still with one eye open. Bob called her. She stretched and strolled calmly out of the crate. She stopped at my feet and peed on me, then followed Bob outside. I stood there with puppy urine running into my shoe, saying, "She's only a puppy, she's only a puppy, she's only a puppy."

Tegan is now five. Our relationship has been a love/hate one. I love her and she hates it. Or she loves me-like barking sweet nothings into my ear when I'm asleep-and I hate it. Many times I've sworn that Tegan would end her days as a wall hanging. But, you know, the little witch is a soul mate.

Patricia Bennett

With your first ADT you have got yourself a new life! Have a lot of fun and never, ever have your tongue between your teeth during play (you'll soon know what I mean). Make yourself a personal "I'm so sorry" routine, that must be performed in a convincing way (try to fake a blush). To illustrate what I mean, I'll give you some stories:

1. The Appendix. I invented my routine when Dina was 3 months old. An elegant lady in a fur coat was passing us. Dina had just finished a poop and I was busy collecting the stuff. Then I heard a whining EEeeeEEe from the lady. When I turned around, the fur coat had got a four legged and very living appendix hanging from the side. I got the appendix off with one hand (the other was holding the poop bag) and did my performance. I didn't get any applause!

2. Chaos In The Obedience Class. Dina was 6-7 months and we were out in the woods practicing the "come" command. On our way

home, we walked past some fenced areas used for agility and obedience classes. In one of them there were ten Shelties doing obedience training. Dina discovered them and couldn't care less about all the "come" training. She ran over and placed herself just outside the gate. Just before I reached her, one of the humans went outside, and Dina went inside. After five minutes of calling, treat promises and chasing, I finally got her. The teacher's face was purple, so I did my "I'm so sorry" performance twice (still no applause).

3. The Purse Snatcher. Dina is 11-12 months old. We are going to pass an elderly woman carrying a purse over her arm. She looks at Dina and smiles at me: "What a nice dog. May I pet her?" "Yes," I said. She reached out her arm to do so. The Nice Dog saw the purse, grabbed it and ran. To the end of the leash. New performance, and this time I almost got applause!

4. The Thief: My wife and I are coming down from a little ski hike in the mountains. Dina is running along at my side. With the exceptions of c*ts and food she is normally very reliable. We are passing a couple sitting in the snow, enjoying the nice weather. In front of them there is an open rucksack. Open rucksack = food! So Dina turns off her hearing aid and runs over to the rucksack. When I get her head out of the sack, she is still chewing. I give her some very well chosen words and two ugly eyes before I do my performance for the couple. No applause, but a sad, understanding look.

Have a nice new life.

Kjell Sjostrom

Pup's Progress

As a youngster, Farah was crate-trained to facilitate housebreaking; and as he began to get the idea, at perhaps 4 months of age, he was confined to the tiled kitchen instead to give him room to stretch out. One day I left him in the kitchen alone for a few hours. Upon my return I found the kitchen doormat out of place in the middle of the floor. Lifting it to put it back by the doorway, I smelled the unmistakable odor of urine. Farah couldn't hold his bladder while I was out; and knowing that he wasn't encouraged to use the floor in the house, he must have dragged the doormat atop the puddle to conceal it. Tricky fellow.

Perhaps a week later, I lifted the doormat from its rightful place by the door in order to sweep the floor. Lo and behold-more urine! That pup figured out how to make his accident practically undetectable: move the doormat, pee, then move it back. We were incredulous.

Farah was growing fast. Soon he was physically old enough to control himself for a longer period of time. The doormat incidents were the last times we cleaned up after him indoors!

Jeanette Sperhac

In the beginning Rhu slept in his crate at night and usually began whimpering about 2:00 a.m. Good sign (doesn't want to soil crate), so I trundle out of bed and stumble to the kitchen door. Bam!! Tassie Marie, the young Old English Sheepdog, bolts through the dogdoor ahead of me, eager to body slam the little prince. No way are we having doggie games at this ungodly hour, so I shuffle to the front door instead, fumbling for the porch lights and gingerly descending the stairs. "Go potty...go ON." Rhu trots over to the shadow of a yew. Is he sitting? Squatting? What IS he doing? I feel like some pervert as I fumble for his little waterspout to ascertain if it's wet or not. Wet-good. Back to bed.

5:15 a.m. Whimpering. Repeat above scenario only this time after he's pottied, I plop him down in the kitchen and prepare to fix his breakfast. The little @#$% is peeing AGAIN amidst the forest of table legs. Tassie's dancing around wanting her breakfast and Rhu looks like any minute he'll start hydroplaning through his self-made puddle. I grab a paper towel and begin to clean up the mess. Rhu takes this as a green light to pull my hair and shake. I push him away and get up for another paper towel. Just enough time for Rhu to make ANOTHER puddle!

Score: Rhu 3, Upright 0

Rhu now sleeps through the night for 8 hours and doesn't soil his crate. Er, until this morning. Because of all the late night outings and interrupted sleep in the last 2 weeks, my immune system is now shot and I'm fighting laryngitis and bronchitis and a sinus infection. I feel LOUSY. Whimper, whimper. It's 4:15 a.m. My own bladder feels ready to explode because of all the fluids I've been drinking. "Hold your horses," I mutter while racing to the bathroom. Too late. By the time I open Rhu's crate door, soggy newspapers surround the shameless beast. And when I swoop him up in my arms, his wet paw flings urine in my eyes.

Score: Rhu 5, Upright 0

Trainer Sherry Karas suggests chanting the mantra "POT-TY, POT-TY" on the rare occasions when P*ss-a-rhu actually has some nitrogen to contribute to the lawn. Religiously I mouth the mantra in an upbeat, happy tone, glad we have no close neighbors. Rhu looks pleased with himself. I also begin rewarding him with a bit of cheese when he potties outdoors. Soon he isn't procrastinating outside too long before doing his duty and then running to me with shiny black eyes, expecting tribute from his upright. Maybe he's making THE connection? Nah. One night when I'm feeling wiped out from dry, hacking coughs, Zak, Tassie, and Rhu all get squirrelly on me at the same time. I have just finished playing nurse to Tassie by cleaning the matted hair from around her "pearl of great vice." I guess I do too good a job for the bristly ends now aggravate her; she begins bouncing her fluffy butt UPANDDOWN UPANDDOWN UPANDDOWN on the kitchen tile, looking as though volts of electricity are forcing her to jiggle; her shaggy head tresses undulate like some animated white mop. Several weeks earlier she'd had to wear a cone around her head when spayed because she has this habit of licking herself raw, so I retrieve the cone and attach it to her collar, thinking she'll settle down in mere moments. CLUNK!! She frantically scrambles to go outside and rams into the dogdoor. "Tassie! Come here!" CLUNK!! She batters my kneecaps. Blindly races towards Zak who skittishly sidesteps her. Then she spins into a sit and continues twirling futilely as though possessed. In the midst of the chaos of trying to shut in Zak and Tassie so Rhu can pee outdoors uninterrupted, Rhu instead pees on the kitchen tile while Tassie blocks the dogdoor with another CLUNK. As I'm running for a paper towel, Zak gets all excited and plops one bear-dale paw in Rhu's puddle-bolting downstairs as I screech. So now there's not just a puddle but a trail to clean.

Score: Rhu 6, Upright 0

"POT-TY OUT-SIDE," I chirp one morning. Rhu yawns sleepily as the birds twitter in the pre-dawn. Then he sits down and just stares at me. I step forward just in time to see pee arcing gracefully between his front feet. He's peeing while sitting down!! Talk about lazy. Thing is, he seems to only pee enough to take the pressure off, not to get empty-is this a guy thing?

Score: Rhu 6, Upright 1

After skimming the chapter on housebreaking in Paul Loeb's book *Smarter Than You Think*, I put Rhu on an 18" tether most of his waking hours so that he can feel a part of the kitchen hubbub and yet he has little room for stealth-peeing. What a relief to be free from hawk-eyed supervision. Rhu doesn't have an accident in 24 hours. It's working!! Yeah! I reward Mr. Cute by removing his tether and allowing him to wrestle 52-pound Tassie. In other words, I let down my guard. Guess what happened 24 hours and 30 minutes into Rhu practicing continence?

Score: Rhu 7, Upright 1

Jadie Davis

(Epilogue: Rhu had a urinary infection and is now on an antibiotic. It's now six days since the initial diagnosis and no noticeable improvement in bladder control yet. Sigh.)

We were getting ready to go out and Ozzie pooped in the house AGAIN! He hasn't had accidents like this since we were housebreaking. This is about the fourth or fifth day in a row that he has done this, and it's getting frustrating! It's cold outside and he's refusing to stay out long enough to go. He'll pee, but not poop (sorry for the technical lingo-comes from having small children). My husband even used the snow blower to make a little dumping area for him. No go! The snow's not even that deep yet-what are we going to do when we get another foot or two?

Because he hasn't been going, we've been keeping him gated in his room to avoid an accident. But he's so pathetic in there that finally we give him the benefit of the doubt and let him out. Five minutes later he's doing his thing on my new oriental rug! Tomorrow we'll be facing the same thing. Any ideas? Should we put our foot down and keep him gated off until he goes outside? He has to learn to tolerate this WI weather. He's got many more years to deal with it!

Roxann and Ozzie in WI

Do you have a crate for him? I am assuming he is under a year old, my guess is between 7 to 9 months old. They seem to slip backwards at that age. Take him outside; tell him to go potty or whatever word you use for P & P. If he doesn't do whichever you expect him to do, bring him back inside and happily put him in his crate and ignore him. Wait an hour or so, then take him back out and wait with him. Do not play with him-this is a business trip. Give him the command again; if he doesn't do as expected after a while, bring him back in and put him in the crate. Follow the procedure till he does what he is supposed to do, then when he does, praise him and bring him in the house. Airedales know that the pathetic looks and whines usually make the owner succumb to the ADT's way, so be firm and withstand the looks and plug your ears. Keep this up for a week or so and he will get the idea that pooping in the house is unacceptable.

Ginny Higdon

Well, seven-week-old Sarah is getting more used to Merlin's attempts at ADT play. She has figured out that when he does the BIGNOSEPOKE and concomitant bark, she had better run to one side (if she's still on her feet). She isn't doing it consistently yet, but she appears to be catching on. This morning she "attacked" Merlin on one of our morning trips to the potty. She waited until Merlin had sat down and was looking the other way. Then she went running (OK, hopping and scampering) right at him and did a MICROBODYSLAM into his right hip, while growling at full puppy volume. Surprisingly, Merlin did not fall over, although Sarah did. (Let's see, Merlin weighs around 82 pounds, and Sarah is maybe 6-8. Yeah Merlin stayed upright OK.) Sarah then got up, barked once, and took off, scampering away from Merlin, obviously hoping for a chase. He followed, NOSEPOKE'd her, knocking her over, of course, and then got a TINYPAWSLAP in the face for his efforts.

Merlin has the run of the house at night, but Sarah is crated. This is actually rather convenient for us, since when we are in bed if Sarah starts to howl, we shake Merlin (huh? whatzit dad? time for breakfast yet? oh. the kid. zzzzzzzzzz.) a few times and send him to see her downstairs and until two days ago she would immediately "talk to Merlin" and hush and then go back to sleep. Did this work Monday and Tuesday nights? No. In fact last night we got a duet out of the deal. Now, in our own defense, I often work until as late as 2:30 or 3:00 in the morning and so Sarah is lying on the carpet, asleep next to my feet when I am. She got in bed around 2:30 on Monday night and 3:15 last night. (Yawn). So her crying for company at 3:40 this morning was not expected. Anyway, her howling sounded like Merlin's familiar AOUOUOUOUOUOUOUO-OOOOOOOOO-UUU UUUUUUUUUU AOUOUUOUOUOUUOUUOUO-OOO-UUU, only about 4 octaves higher. I will try to tape her tonight to get a reminder tape.

Yes. Mornings I take Merlin and Sarah out to the potty about 6:00. When I get up, I now slip on some sweatpants and a sweatshirt before going out, along with some soccer sandals. Now when we go out, Merlin is on a flexi-lead, but Sarah is off lead. This morning, she followed OK, but holding onto my sweatpants while growling and shaking them all the way. At one point she let go, jumped as high on my leg as she could, got a better grip on my sweatpants and commenced the same kill-the-cloth trick as before. I quickly had to adjust my holding of Merlin's lead then, because-have I mentioned losing over 70 pounds in the last year and my clothes getting loose? -she pulled my sweatpants off. After that I carried her for a while.

What else? Well last night she managed to steal 3 dish towels (not her frozen teething towels), Merlin's new ball, some spaghetti, Nicholas's sneaker, a pencil, and some other, undistinguished junk. That was just one hour's activity. Also, she is starting to try to play with Merlin. I had forgotten how early Merlin did AIRESNAPS, but she is already doing them-you can hear them all the way upstairs when she does one in the living room. Oh well, when she looks up with those little black eyes and that cute little black nose, it is easy to forgive a lot.

William W. Austin

Rhu has evolved into a Mr. Woofer wannabe. Hardened criminal type. He crafts the timing of his "accident" to coordinate with his P.O.Y. (p*ss on you) attitude. This morning I just finished scrubbing and mopping the kitchen floor for an hour and a half. Let Rhu out of the dog room long enough to feed him lunch. Then I hustled Tassie up beside me on the kitchen bench to have my photo taken with her so that I could have it posted on the sheepie list. WHAT ABOUT MEEEEEEEE? nosed Whiz Kid (HOP, HOP, HOP, BOING, BOING, BOING on his hind feet while trying to squirm into my lap). "No Rhu! Off! I said OFF!" Sigh. "Okay, you little egocentric terrorist, time-out in the dog room," I mutter as I ignominiously hustle him by his collar. "Why don't you go outside and potty?" I ask brightly to distract him. Uh-oh. I said the "p" word. "And I do mean OUTSIDE!" The juvenile delinquent quietly peeeeeeered through the dog door grate. Then he played limp rag doll when I grabbed him by the scruff, SHAME, SHAME, SHAMED him by glowering darkly into his subdued eyes-eyes that appeared to be mentally dissociating himself from his present circumstances. He has the attitude of the slave girl Prissy in Gone With the Wind (1939). The battle is just outside Atlanta, Melanie is in hard labor, and Scarlett is furiously barking orders to Prissy to seek help. Prissy meanders down the staircase singing off-key, "La-de-da-de-da" out of sync with her mistress' agenda. That's Rhu. La-de-da. Dumb like a fox.

Jadie Davis

Question: How do we stop our puppy from biting everything that comes in close proximity to her mouth?

Give her a rope bone or Booda bone as an alternative to human limbs and so on. The floss bones are better and last longer. You can soak any of them in water and freeze them to help ease her discomfort when she starts teething and they are washable.

Pick up a couple of Kongs-they are conical shaped hard rubber chew toys. Get the large and the king sizes. The puppy will grow into them! Put a biscuit inside them or smear some peanut butter deep inside one and some cheese deep in the other. These toys will keep the puppy busy in her crate playing "Aardvark." The Kong is also the only toy I would leave with a puppy while it is unattended. (Ed. note: some people have found that the Kong is also the only safe-while-unattended toy for adult dogs, too.)

Deanna Lulik

Fear of Loud Noises

Don't try to soothe her fears by sweet-talking her or petting her. Act as if nothing happened. Trying to calm her down will only reinforce her fear. Do you have any other dogs there? Are they noise-proofed? They may go about their merry way, and she will see how they react. If not, then you'll have to take time to desensitize her to loud noises.

I have to get my pups used to gunfire. Not all of them take to it, and sometimes I have to really work on them. Katie, the

Goldenslayer (obedience term, not really out killing goldens) was gunshy, so I started desensitizing her with a plain old paper lunch bag. Start out by teasing her with it, like you would play with a squeaky toy, or something-rustle it, whap it, crinkle it up-all the time being a bit noisy with it. Then let her have it as a reward. Let her tear it to smithereens. This is the most important part! You are reward-ing them for the fearLESSness! As each "play" session progresses, work your way up the noise scale, eventually slapping the paper bag. The last step is to blow air into it and pop it, really quick and after making the most noise during the session. Do NOT ever just go in and pop a bag one day. It's all a series of build-ups. AND DON'T FORGET TO GIVE HER A REWARD!

One additional note: get her out to all kinds of places. Socialization will be the best thing for her. If you have no other dogs, go out with friends who have "steady" dogs. Go for walks with them, go to minimally noisy places first. Don't overdo it! Build your way up to noisier places and be sure to act as if nothing is wrong when you hear a loud noise.

'Dale Burrier

Puppy Grooming

Handling a pup's mouth frequently is very useful indeed-it makes the doggy toothbrush routine possible, as well as easy dosing with pills. My Airedale is on medication now; he is simple to dose thanks to the mouth handling we've done. Twice a day I call him into the kitchen with the words "Time for your medicine." He sits politely and lets me coax open his jaws, place a pill at the back of his tongue, and stroke his throat until he swallows. After each pill he gets a treat: some bread, or a biscuit.

I only wish we had taught him to have his temperature taken! Last time he was at the vet's, he backed his butt into the corner with a terrible growl when the technician tried to insert the thermometer. I can't say that I blame him.

Jeanette Sperhac

Zoe is now 4 months and loves to be brushed up on the desk/makeshift grooming table: We have a grooming ritual that seems to work. Her treat is KIX cereal (low in sugar). I started by putting her on top of a high surface (desk or grooming table) while holding her collar. I tell her "good girl" and give her a treat, about one each minute while I just pet her and rub her tummy. Then my son Jake, who is almost 5, stands there and gives her a treat while I brush her. Now, a few months later, she just responds to the "good girl." We always brush in the same location in the house, so she knows what to expect when I hoist her up there. She will have NOTHING to do with the brush, comb, etc. when she is on the floor.

Kari Stielow

Encounters

My little neck of the desert is infested with a particularly nasty weed known as the Foxtail. Foxtails are hell on Airedales; those woolly chaps that sophisticated folks call "furnishings" act like a magnet for the nasty little darts the foxtail weed uses to perpetuate its existence.

During his first summer with us, Mr. Woofer got into the damn things out back of the house, as I hadn't the time to get out my trusty flame-thrower and send those foxtails to hell where they belong. Before long, his toes had blown up to the size of sausages from embedded foxtails. We tried digging them out with surgical tools but even a pint-sized ADT puppy was more than Doctors Jenny and Chuck could manage when the patient didn't want to be treated. Finally, when we were both a pint shy of blood from the wounds Mr. Woofer had inflicted on us in protest of our amateur surgery, we decided to cut our losses and take him to the vet.

"I don't really like to give anesthesia to puppies," the vet told us. "I think I can just hold him down and -OW! DAMMIT!-on second thought, I will give him anesthesia...." We left Mr. Woofer to the vet's ministrations and went out to dinner. When we returned, the foxtails had been removed and the swelling abated; but now we had to contend with a stoned puppy. Mr. Woofer thought he could negotiate those stairs outside the vet's office but his legs had other ideas.

Ever see a pup do a triple somersault down the steps? The things you see when you don't have your camera....

Chuck Shaddoway

Madison, as usual, followed me into the bathroom today. In the past, the bathroom has provided great entertainment for her with toilet paper to swipe, toilet flushing noises, a puppy in the mirror-her eyes say it is there but her sniffer says she is the only dog in the room, how confusing-so she trots in there frequently.

Today the item of choice was the door stopper spring. She bumped into it a couple of days ago and investigated the phenomenon then. Today she slapped it with her paws and grabbed it with her mouth, trying to get the biggest, loudest TWAANG she could. I scooted her little butt out of there after I got over laughing but I have a feeling she'll be back to visit that toy again.

Trish Ganter

My husband and I had the opportunity to foster a five-month-old male, Truman, for a month as ATRA (Airedale Terrier Rescue & Adoption) volunteers. It was love at first sight for us and our three adolescent female ADTs, Ivy, Annie, and Poppy. It was fun to watch this puppy mill, store reject, experience snow, stairs, furniture, shoes, chew toys, the TV and constant attention for the first time. He hadn't been outdoors in months!

The girls did the training. When they went out to do their business, Truman followed; so housebreaking was a snap, except he squatted instead of lifting his leg like a male. When they sat for cookies, Truman followed their lead and did the same. By week three, we were pretty proud of the job we had done.

The funny thing about this little guy was how he captured the heart of our Ivy. She never left his side in spite of his puppy biting, wanting to eat her food, and rough housing. Ivy is our dominant female, so no one fools around with her without checking if it's OK. Ivy is one of those ADTs that's "in your face." She's first at the door, first to eat dinner, first in the car, first to go in or out the door. She's fairly intelligent but she refuses to bark at the door to come in. She leaves that to the other dogs. Even Truman caught on to that one.

One day when I let the Silly Sisters and Truman out for a run around the yard, I watched out my window while working on the computer. They'd fly by in one direction and back the other. Life was wonderful for this canine collective. My thoughts drifted back to the computer screen. Suddenly, I heard an unusual sound. It was an unfamiliar ADT bark coming from the yard, not a puppy bark but a deep ADT bark-yelling at me. It was imploring me to come. Jolted back to reality, I looked out the window but couldn't see who was calling. I got up and ran to the back door. There was Ivy, the one who never barks at the door, bouncing and barking. I went into the yard and she ran with me to find Truman had caught his collar on the fence. (Don't ask me how; it's one of those puppy things.)

Truman was freed and Ivy was all over him, doting like a mother. She made him come inside and followed him everywhere. I don't know what it was about this little guy but he melted the queen bee's heart. We've fostered other dogs here but only Truman cast this spell on Ivy. It was true, full-time devotion. I can't explain it. Normally Annie is our nurturer but she couldn't have cared less; she found Truman fairly annoying. We don't know if Ivy would act the same way if we fostered a puppy again but we found out something about her true colors in time of need.

Now that he's gone to his permanent home, she still won't bark to come in!

Patty Eisenbruan

"They" say, to discourage countersurfing, wastebasket browsing, and the like, to place snap trap mousetraps on the table, counter, or wastebasket. When the dog touches the counter, the loud noise of the trap and hint of physical harm (though only their egos are bruised) will teach the dog not to go there. Also, they're effective when you're not around and the lesson holds no negative associations with you.

Yeah, right.

Within a couple of tries, baby Moxie figured out how to discharge the trap without sustaining bodily injury, then grab the trap and run through the house with it, in a full-blown TUCKBUTTRUN. Can't you just hear her saying, "Neh, neh, neh, neh neh, can't pull this one on me!"

Ronna Miller

PS I have caught her on multiple occasions trying to help herself to ice cubes from the fridge door dispenser. She is tall enough to reach but not quite tall enough to push the button, yet. Now, if we could only teach her to pour the tequila without spilling....

Quite by accident, we have given Zoe a great new "toy." I picked up several fleece, car washing mitts at Costco for the car washers in the family. Before our son even got his wet, Zoe snatched it up and gleefully ran off with it. She tossed it, caught it, "killed" it, chased it and was so thoroughly delighted with her new toy that our son used the traditional rags and relinquished the mitt. Since that day, Zoe has chewed off the cuff, but left the fleece mitt intact. She plays with it daily. When I'm going out, I stuff it with other toys and a few treats. The investment of about $3.00 (Canadian) has paid off big time. It is her favorite toy. Stuffed or unstuffed it is also great for playing fetch, either inside or outside. It damages neither flowers nor furniture.

Anne Clarke

When Tegan was a puppy, about 8 months, she came flying down the stairs and hit one of the wrought iron posts full speed. Popped the 4 ft rail, sending it flying, never even her slowed down. She rounded the corner and took a flying leap onto my chest (I was half asleep in the recliner watching TV).

My lungs came out to discuss this event with me and to express their displeasure at being so rudely interrupted from their important task of supplying oxygen to my body. I conveyed my total agreement by a series of frantic hand gestures. The lungs agreed to re-enter my body and I agreed to move the recliner. This was a comprise. They wanted Tegan's hide nailed to the wall. A sentiment that I could understand, but at the time I was busy trying to stuff the lungs back down each ear.

In typical husband fashion, Bob came down stairs (the chair and I were overturned and I now matched the color: blue) and started to explain to me in that "kind, long suffering voice" that I shouldn't encourage Tegan to get on my lap; she was too big for that now. He then wanted to know if the chair was broken (it's his favorite), and if I was done watching TV so that could he could change the channel.

I was lying face down on the floor stuffing my lungs back in and Tegan was bouncing on my back, barking at them. Since I wasn't answering him he decided to put the dog outside and then came back in the living room. I am still on the floor gasping. He finally asks me if I am all right. My white knuckle crawl to his leg-I was trying to bite his ankle-was taken as an affirmative.

Fortunately for him, he then saw the broken rail and moved out of my reach, mumbling about me and MY crazy dog. I remained on the floor plotting my revenge. But that's another story.

Pat Bennett

Chewing

When Brandy was about five months old she was suddenly quiet one evening. Doris and I both realized this about the same time. I headed up stairs to see what our wonderful pup was doing. Well there at the top of the stairs in her best ADT playbow was Brandy. In her mouth were several pieces of coloured paper. There was a lot of green paper, some purple and some blue paper. (Note: Americans are always accusing us Canadians of having "funny coloured money.") Instantly I realized the severity of the situation! As I approached Brandy, she was convinced that the games were about to begin. But I-the smart upright-wasn't having any of that. I approached the issue less dramatically-she wasn't going to win this one. This is what we'd been told in puppy classes.

This approach had a serious down side however. As I pretended to ignore her she continued to chew. But I knew if I made a grab for her and missed all bets would be off. Finally, Doris appeared on the scene and distracted Brandy and I grabbed her collar! I pried open the Jaws of Death and extracted 2 twenty dollar bills (green), one $10 (purple) and one $5 (blue). The rest of my wallet was on the living room floor virtually untouched. (Brandy had been counter surfing on the dresser.) Since I had to work the next day and I hate confrontation (a.k.a embarrassment) I gave the shredded paper to Doris and SHE had to explain it all to the bank teller the following day! Luckily, the money was exchanged with very few questions. (Just in case, Doris had Brandy in the car willing to give any bank officer who didn't believe the story a demonstration if needed.)

Rick Williams

I want to reiterate the wonders of asparagus. One of the nurses in the vet's office remarked how good my little staple-guzzler looked. As you may recall, she had swallowed 4 large industrial staples a month ago and they all were expelled the next day with the aid of canned asparagus, which wrapped around the staples and eased them through her system. In the conversation the nurse emphasized that fresh don't work nearly as well as canned. She added that a dog expelled a whole chicken carcass with the aid of two cans of whole (not chopped) asparagus with a bit of fat added to make it enticing.

Susan Olsen

When Daisy was about 7 months old she ate an entire disposable shaver, a pink Daisy shaver. Anyway, after x-rays we could see that the two blades from the shaver were indeed in her stomach.

Panic set in: surgery!! YIKES! $$$$$$$$$ However, this was Friday night; we had until Monday afternoon for her to pass them. The vet had us feed her the following in order for it to pass without cutting her up: hamburger meat, a spoonful of Metamucil, castor oil (I think, now I don't even remember). Anyway, this mix makes the poop like a sausage. A coating on the outside with everything tucked in it. Sorry, if this is a little too graphic.

The next day the vet gave her something to try and throw it up. Sure enough one blade came up stuck to a piece of carpet. (Thank goodness she was chewing the rug.) To make a long weekend story short, the second piece finally passed through her that Monday. If anyone would have seen me, what a sight. Digging around in the dog's poop then jumping up and down, dancing and carrying on with a little blade in my gloved hand. What an ordeal. She's almost 3 now and has never been back into the bathroom garbage.

Daphne Rhodes

We had some friends over for dinner the other night and after dinner were playing cards out on the deck (we live right over the Pacific Ocean and the sunsets are particularly colorful this time of year). Fancy was under the table while we were concentrating on the game. When our friends got up to leave, Bob shouted "She's been chewing my shoe! These cost me $175.00!" My husband said, "Oh, don't worry, she cost $700.00." Is that Airedale-owner reasoning-or what? Afterward my husband said that he couldn't believe (A) the guy didn't know his foot was being gnawed alive in the first place, and (B) anyone with such a bourgeois/materialistic sense of reality shouldn't spend $175.00 on a pair of shoes if they were worried about "worldly damage" to them. Go Tony!

Barbara and Tony Saia

It's consoling to know that there are other Airedales out there wreaking destruction. However, I can't believe any have reached Havoc's standard as yet. He has destroyed one Easy Spirit shoe (expensive), managed to squeeze into a closet and chew the corner off of a good quilt, strew toilet paper all over the house, terrorize the cats, and, when put outside, pulled up three poinsettias that I have been nurturing since last Christmas and scattered a whole bag of potting soil over the patio. That's just this morning! Short of crating him there is no barricade that can keep him confined.

Ordinarily I keep better watch on him but we're leaving to spend the weekend at Big Bear and I have been busy trying to think of what I need to pack for the dogs and me. Oh well, I keep telling myself that a mischievous puppy is an intelligent puppy. And certainly everything I've noted about him bears out his intelligence.

Jean Wilson

Teddy must have been related! In the first two years I had him, he ate about 10 area rugs, gnawed the paint off radiators and, in my favorite escapade, went up to a perfectly flat painted wall and used his front teeth to scrape the paint off that. At age 2 he suddenly and mercifully grew up and stopped most of this. I saved some of the area rugs that had holes in them and pulled them out again for the others' terrible puppyhoods figuring it wouldn't matter if they ate them. But no, Newton the WFT preferred pens and expensive eyeglasses. Toby liked the nailed-down carpet and any kind of paper, especially toilet paper, Kleenex and books. Preferably a very expensive library book. Teddy taught me the benefit of crates. But I always lost something when I started experimenting with leaving the guys loose. Toby at 3 still nibbles on the toilet roll now and then just to show he knows I was gone!

Mary Jane Smetanka

It's the sport of thieving that Katie loves! Last night, I took her for only a short walk. I guess she didn't think I had given her enough of my time, because when we got home, she harassed me for a half hour or more! I was in the kitchen; she tried to bite at the refrigerator door handle. Then she attempted to chew on the woodwork. Now, mind you, she's looking straight at me when she does all this, just trying to push my buttons! It's really hilarious. Now this morning, she stole a Fisher Price toy from our grandson's stash. Usually she just tosses this stuff around until I get the drift that it's not her toy she's playing with, but today, she proceeded to munch the handle off and spit out the pieces-luckily! When I removed it, she tore back to try to score another toy! There's a pan of brownies cooling in the kitchen. Uh, oh, it's kinda quiet out there-gotta go!

Christie Hansen

I. Our Libby dog hates Barbies. If my little daughter leaves her door ajar, Libby searches until she finds one, looks that Barbie in the eye, and very deliberately chews off the right hand. It's happened five times now, and it's always the right hand! The Christmas Barbie didn't even last one whole day, and Libby amputated right up past her elbow in three small bites. The other creepy thing is that she doesn't even eat the hands-just leaves them as not-so-gentle reminders of her opinions.

II. While my brother was visiting recently, he and our Airedale, Libby, became fast friends. Libby's 11 months old, and we've had her for 2 months. The day before my brother left, he asked me if I'd seen his leather cap (very important to him-we once turned back and fished it out of the Columbia River after it flew off during a boat ride). I hadn't seen it. He asked me whether Libby would have swiped it. I told him I didn't think so. So he and I went to the guest room to search around the room, in his suitcase, and under the bed. Libby followed us, stayed long enough to see what we were doing, and then left. My brother and I were still looking for the cap when she trotted back into the room. She was carrying the cap in her mouth and dropped it at his feet! I love this Airedale.

Mary Melton

It is hard to get through that chewing puppy stage. Make sure that there are plenty of doggie toys for the pup. Try and puppy proof the house as much as possible. Watch the pup closely. When they started to pick up something they weren't supposed to chew, we said "achhhhhhh" loudly to our pups and then gave them something that was ok to chew.

A tired dog is a happy, good dog, so I would think lots of exercise would be helpful. When you can't watch a puppy, consider training it to be in a crate or an ex-pen. Some puppies chew from boredom, some because they are just in that puppy stage and some just like to chew. Even our boy Bailey who chewed off zillions of cedar shingles from our old house (we sold it before it fell apart) has stopped chewing for the most part.

Susan Sheehan

CHAPTER SEVEN
Airedales at Play

BEING SMART DOGS on the whole, Airedales like to keep busy, whether playing typical doggie games like Dig to Australia and Steal the Socks, or helping their people perform humble household tasks such as cooking. If you run out of ideas, this chapter will suggest ways to keep your dogs entertained.

Havoc has always insisted on helping me in everything I do, whether it is sweeping the floor, feeding the fish, untying shoes, fetching the newspaper, preparing food, eating food (I do keep proclaiming that I need to diet), etc. But yesterday he took his assistance one step too far. As I was leaning over the fish pond trying to scoop out some leaves, Havoc rushed up, eager as always to participate, causing me to lose my balance and hurl into the pond. He, of course, delightedly joined me. Both of us emerged festooned with algae and slime. Sometimes I think he tries too hard to live up to his name.

Jean Wilson

Ernie has discovered a new way to antagonize the cranky neighbor dog through the fence without her having time to climb over it. He runs along it barking joyously in her face while she keeps pace with him on the other side, snarling like she's going to eat him alive. The neighbors and I are pretty even-keeled about the whole thing, so it's more of a roll your eyes and scold the dogs kind of thing. Once the fence is eliminated (as when the neighbor dog climbs it and ends up in our yard) the argument is usually over. She also likes to attack our lawnmower through the fence as well. I just have to laugh, almost, when dogs get this bee in their bonnet and you just can't convince them what they're fussing about is not important. Ernie seems to take a great ego boost from it, in any case (that must be the real ADT in him coming out).

Paula Coyne

Nora also loves to torment the dogs next door; they are Husky-Golden Lab mixes. The girls next door have dug a little hole under the fence, just enough to stick a nose or paw through. Whenever Nora finds a particularly attractive stick, or is really into her tennis ball, she will dash over to the hole, shake her prize in front of it, and then haul butt away from the fence!

Dawn Endean

Mine are impossible to get back in the house when there is blowing snow. They love it. The first winter I lived in Ohio, we had the great blizzard of January, 1978. Lucy, my first all-my-own Airedale, was 5 months old. She spent most of the blizzard day galloping around the back yard chasing snow flakes and the last few leaves being blown out of the trees. She would only come in when the ice balls between her toes got so big they were uncomfortable. She would stay in just long enough to drop them on the floor underfoot, then would ask to go out again.

After the wind and snow quit and we had ten-foot drifts, she and I played endlessly in the snow. She loved to be picked up and bodily tossed into a drift and would do major TUCKBUTTRUNS after she dug herself out.

Barbara Mann

We've just come in from a winter walk; the snow was falling, soft and fine like icing sugar. It was wonderful. No one else had braved the 18 degree F temperature and we had the park to ourselves. And, oh, how these dales loved it! They relish the cold and snow. They act like pups, running, jumping, tails tucked between their legs-enticing each other to playfight-up a hill and down the ravine-playing catch me if you can, then rolling in the snow to make Aire angels. Their coats get packed with snow, frosty eyebrows and big black leather noses poking out from icicle beards. Chelsea searches for field mice under snow-covered tufts of grass and Winston searches for other nice smells which still linger on the bushes and trees. He rescues an old tennis ball which he proudly brings to me for safekeeping.

On the homeward path, on go the leashes and they slow down, not wanting the walk to end. Once we get to the small park down the street, they perk up again, pouncing in the snowdrifts which surround the skating rink, kicking up snow and grabbing each other's leashes to see who can pull the hardest. When we finally reach the house, all of a sudden they are cold. They start lifting feet, not being able to decide which foot is the coldest. They hurry into the house and stand in the kitchen, waiting for the ice and snow to melt in pools around their feet. They pretend to hate being toweled dried, but lean into the towels, no doubt in a hurry to sleep by the fire. They smell clean and fresh (and wet!), but they are happy with their walk and content to curl up for a snooze and probably dream of new snow games to play.

Helen Arnold

A few years ago we had more than two feet of snow on the ground. Although Geoffrey enjoyed romping through it, he didn't want to hunker down and poop. I solved the problem by shoveling a path to his favorite spot and then clearing an area about the size of a football field! He would trot right out, do his business and then trot back to the house, or perhaps go for a romp through the snow.

Karl Broom

About a year ago, I got suckered into buying one of those grooming mitts. I'm sure you know the one "as seen on TV." It is made of canvas and has a rubber palm with little raised rubber nubs on it. It is supposed to be good for stroking your dog or cat to remove dead hair. Well, until now I have found it pretty useless for either Airedales or cats. However, guess what it is REALLY good at? I discovered today (necessity is the mother of invention) that it is really good at removing all the snow and ice from Airedale furnishings. It really excels at this. If there are any other listers out there who bought this expensive "grooming aid" and threw it into a corner, get it out and put it to good use!

Gitte Koopmans

Max, in his heyday, loved to sproing off the stairs from half-way up as a prelude to the race around the main floor. With my hooman intelligence, I decided that all I had to do to stop this trick was to stand at the bottom of the stairs and make myself as big as possible (wave arms, etc.) What fun! He launched right at me-grinning all the way! I dropped to the ground and he sailed right over. Guess who got trained! The only thing I can say in my defense is that Max is my first (but not my last) Airedale.

Jan Bryant

I never had a 'dale that didn't love sticks. Spook loved to run with them, dive for them, carry them, and bury them. When we first brought Leia home and became a 2-dog family, I knew it was going to work between Leia and Roxy when Leia, who was tied out in the back yard so far she could only touch noses with Roxy, went into the woods and brought a REALLY BIG STICK to share. Actually it was a log about 3 inches in diameter and about 12 feet long. She spent an hour dragging it out of the woods, up the hill and then po-sitioning it so that she and Roxy could both chew on it at the same time. That very day I called Leia's former owner and told her Leia was a keeper.

My firewood is migratory, frequently rearranged by 'dales. And some of it is 10" in diameter. Having said all that, I would like to take this opportunity to remind us all that chewing on sticks is not a good idea and I try hard to discourage it these days. On Wednesday August 7 1991 (notice its such a vivid memory I still know the day and date), I noticed that not only had Leia not eaten any food for two days but she wanted to drink but couldn't. I made a rush trip to Pet

Emergency in the middle of the night. She had a splinter embedded in her tongue. It was so swollen she could not swallow, was completely dehydrated and close to death. Vet said if I'd waited till morning she might not have made it. She was such a stoic I'm amazed I caught it at all. Don't let your precious Airedales chew sticks.

Alaska Carol S. Dickinson

I bought my Teddy a chew man 4 years ago (I can't believe it is that long) and he still loves it. He softly gnaws on it for about 10-15 minutes, then I hear a big sigh; he rolls onto his side and falls asleep with the chew man as his pillow. Holly prefers a hedgehog toy which she sneaks outside; and then I accidentally run over it with the lawnmower, so she has been through about five of them. The dogs never tear them up.

Geri Lowe

Our (mine and Teddy's-no one else likes the slime and mud when it is tossed in their lap!) favorite toy is a 6" diameter heavy rubber ring. This can be rolled along the ground for chasing and picking up while its still rolling, as a modified Frisbee, as something to use to play "ring the tail of the Airedale," as a handy muzzle, and more. He has had his for seven years and it still looks good. I pop it through the dishwasher from time to time. This is a great puppy toy. Teddy spent about two weeks learning to pick it up when it was flat on the ground. He couldn't get his teeth around it but eventually learned to press a paw down on the outside edge and quickly grab the opposite side as it came up. It was fun to watch-he spent hours perfecting this!

Ellana Livermore

It sounds as though everybody has a lot better luck with soft fluffy toys that I do. I haven't had an Airedale yet that wasn't capable of destroying a fleece toy in minutes. They all absolutely love them, and carry them and throw them around very proudly like little prey; but at my house they are doled out only when I can devote my undivided attention, because I have to watch my girls very carefully and remind them to be gentle. They start with little nibbles, and before I know it, an arm, leg, eye, nose, whatever (or the stuffing) has been removed. Especially with two Airedales, they both always want the same fleece toy, which then becomes a not very durable tug toy!

Gitte Koopmans

That's how my guys are, too. Toby absolutely dotes on fleece toys, so I have spent a fortune on them. Right now we have two 9-inch fleece balls and four 4-inch ones in various corners of the house. Having lots of them around seems to diminish the concentrated gutting of one particular ball and cuts down on fights between the guys over a toy. However, I am constantly sewing them up and re-placing the stuffing, whereupon Toby immediately finds the place where I stitched and rips it out again. Newton loves to go for the squeakers inside so I have to watch that. At the moment they are all either pierced by canine teeth or taken out.

Mary Jane Smetanka

Kugel and I have an airport appointment this evening to pick up my family from another of their worldly jaunts. We are regulars at the international terminal and she has a small following of airport employees who go out of their way to say hello and pet her. I tie colorful balloons to the back of Kugel's harness on long ribbons and she parades around like a true clown! Imagine an ADT at the international gate with a halo of balloons on long, ribbon-like antennae in the center of her back! She makes it very easy for my family to find us. Kugel explodes with jumps, dances and circles of delight upon greeting the family at the gate. The balloons spin in all directions-last time she was a splash of muted pastels. In the meanwhile, she entertains everyone awaiting their families with Airedale tricks and obedience games. Kids especially seem to enjoy her.

Kiwi (Debbi) Carley

The first time we took my new car (now three years old) to the beach for the weekend, we discovered a "design flaw." The car, a

Honda Prelude, has the emergency flasher button on the console just in front of the gearbox between the bucket seats.

Bonnie was already grumbling about being crammed into the rear compartment. When we stopped to get lunch, she climbed into the driver's seat so she could guard the car; of course she stepped on the emergency flashers. We took a window seat in the restaurant to keep an eye on the car and had to take turns going back to turn the flashers off. In fact, for the whole trip she found it an excellent way to get us to come back to the car. She KNEW we didn't want the battery to run down and it was the perfect way to get lots of attention. She enjoyed the fact that everyone passing by the car in the parking lot would look in at her wondering what kind of emergency that big fuzzy dog was having.

Judy Dwiggins

Our town is pretty dog-friendly and we go into many stores with Teddy. In fact, she often stalls in front of favorite stores and urges me to go in. Some of them do have cookies, but not all the one she seems to find interesting do. She definitely enjoys all the oos and ahhhs, not that she particularly wants to be petted by strangers. Strange dog.

When she was a pup, she used to stall in the middle of the sidewalk every time a bunch of college-aged girls were coming in her direction. She just loves women, and she knew they were likely to ooo and ahh over her lovely puppiness. If it were a bunch of rowdy college boys, she used to bark. Now she mostly just gives them a glare of suspicion.

Kanako Ohara

I just got back from the dog park. Today was a beautiful day, so the park was very busy with many different types of dogs all interacting quite nicely. All of a sudden, in comes a little beagle with enough energy for ten dogs. He entices a group of about five or six to play "catch me if you can." There were a couple of hound mixes, a Doberman, another mix of some sort, and my 'dale, Hannah. After a few rounds of fast paced tag with everyone following directly behind the beagle, Hannah, brilliant Airedale that she is, decided to cut the beagle off at the pass, whereby she had to leap over him in order not to body slam him head on. This she did several times. The idea was not to catch the little guy, but to prove she could do it, and she did. Even after seeing the brilliance of it all, no one else followed suit. I am always amazed and continue to profess the awesome intelligence of our beloved Airedales!

Sandi Cooley

Here in Portland there are two or three city parks that have a fenced area designated as off-lead dog heaven. We are lucky to have one about 10 minutes away that is roughly 10 acres of open lawn. The city provides bags and trash facilities. Normally it's a great place for exercise and socialization; dogs and people wander in and out all day and there is almost always somebody ready for a game of keep-away or just tearing around.

Yesterday was extra special. It was the official Halloween celebration at our park. When we arrived, there were approximately 35 dogs of all shapes and sizes, some in costume, as well as plenty of humans with bags of treats. Tricks seemed to be optional. Fiona showed her "only child" status by pushing to the front of every group in which treats were being handed out. Of course, the funny part was when these people apologized for spoiling her dinner. As if!

Mary Heinricher

CHAPTER EIGHT
Creative Training

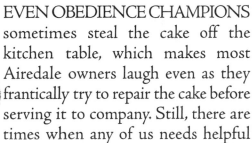

EVEN OBEDIENCE CHAMPIONS sometimes steal the cake off the kitchen table, which makes most Airedale owners laugh even as they frantically try to repair the cake before serving it to company. Still, there are times when any of us needs helpful advice. Do not look here for instructions on how to teach your Airedale to sit or come when called. Instead you'll read how Sidney taught her dogs to behave during bath time, Linda's guide to finding a boarding kennel and making your dog comfortable there, various methods for prying open the JAWSOFDEATH when the "drop it" command does not work, and plenty of wry comments on ADT behavior. As for obedience competition, Yvonne Michalak writes, "I don't know if we'll ever win any titles but we sure have fun."

Who Dun Its Charlie Chan was the number one Airedale in obedience in the Front and Foremost system two years in a row, 1997 and 1998; number 3 out of all the terriers for 1997 (placement for 1998 not known by printing time), and number one Airedale in obedience in Canada for 1998. Charlie was the first male Airedale to earn his AKC-UDX, the first Airedale to earn a UKC-UD, and was very close to earning his UKC-OTCH when he died. He had his States Kennel Club CDX, and ASCA-CDX. High Terrier awards, High Airedale awards, High in trials, and High combined- he has earned several of all of them.

He was an extremely well-loved Airedale who was a wonderful ambassador for the breed. He did his stay exercises with his tail continuously wagging. It was his trademark. It made a lot of judges very nervous that he would break his stay, but no, he just kept looking to his left and right as if to say to the other dogs, "Isn't this fun," and then look forward and continue to wag his tail. He loved working and wagged his tail like a timer till the exercise was finished. There was one time he wagged his tail the entire time on the long stand for examine which was over 6 minutes long. His whole body was wagging, but his feet never moved! The judge loved it and just smiled at me! There were so many wonderful funny things Charlie did. I miss him so very much. There wasn't a day that went by, that he didn't make me laugh!

Sandy Schmitz, Charlie's owner, handler, and partner

Charlie died unexpectedly on 25 June, 1999. His and Sandy's friend Nancy Foster writes: Sandy Schmitz and Charlie Airedale were working partners. Charlie was a young seven and had achieved more obedience titles than any other Airedale in history. Sandy had worked hard and Charlie had learned his lessons well.

Agility

Once you teach them to jump and reward them for jumping, you have big problems. Drew takes off over the fence now and stands on the other side thinking he is so good and clever because he can jump. He has not figured out how to get back in, however; so yesterday after he jumped out, I brought hot dogs out for the girls and he watched me give treats but was afraid to jump back in. I guess he is not the sharpest knife in the drawer but he is funny and very handsome.

Joanne Helm

Giving Meds.

Montgomery, who takes medication regularly for his Scleritis and also gets Derm Tabs daily, is a real trooper. He either gets his pills in liverwurst, cream cheese or peanut butter. Or when in doubt, drop it on the floor and yell, "Don't you take that." Sure enough, he lunges for it and it's gone! He also gets eye drops daily. When he was first diagnosed, the vet warned us that he would probably need drops every day for the rest of his life so we had better make it good. Well, they gave us a lemon and we made lemonade. When I tell him to come for his drops he comes, will sit directly in front of me, and tilt his head (this is the only time he is this cooperative). He lets me put the drops in, and I massage around the eye a little, plant a big kiss on his big nose, rub his head and ears and off he goes. It really is a special time for us and he definitely looks forward to it.

Roe & Roger Quinn

At the Groomer's

Today I took Indiana to a grooming shop where I'm hoping to get a job. The owner, who is the friendliest person, asked that I bring my dog in to groom so that she could see my technique. Well, Indiana didn't think today was a good day for any of this; he barked nonstop and fidgeted! After his bath, I put him in the drying crate and he not only pooped but pooped a glass marble! He had obviously stolen it from my son's room.

I cleaned the poop, took him outside, put him back on the table, and while I was finishing drying him, he started to pee. I finished what I could and left. Usually I put a prong collar on him but this time used just the leather one because I really wanted to get out of there. He jumped off the seat of the van and out the door before I even got in. He ran toward a busy road, ignoring my commands, then looped around, doubled back, and ran past the front window of the grooming shop.

On his way past the window the second time, the owner came out and, feeling one inch tall, I grabbed his leash and dragged him off to the van where I chastised him all the way home. I dropped him off, changed quickly, and went off to a doctor's appointment where they couldn't understand why my blood pressure was up.

Indiana normally does not act this way. I swear he did it on purpose. Thanks for letting me vent. Now it's kind of funny.

Mary Anne Pokorny

(Note: see the puppy chapter for other grooming information)

The Bath

I've been clicking and treating the boys for getting in the tub for about six months. It is right next to the pot, so they get lots of practice. The payoff came today with bath time (I don't bathe them very often, obviously). Jack, who would run away whenever he saw me get the bath things together, didn't exactly jump for joy, but he allowed me to lead him to the tub without struggling and hopped in on his own.

The other things that have made bath time much easier are the suction-cup leash and the hand-held nozzle that I have attached where the shower head used to be. The dog came out thoroughly clean and rinsed, I was able to do that tricky soaping and rinsing around the eyes and ears, I actually wore clothes and shoes and didn't get wet, there was hardly a drop outside the tub AND I was able to do a major towel-down with the dog in the tub instead of having my furniture take the brunt.

Jack actually looked like he might be enjoying it, although he wouldn't admit it to me. Something to remember is that a dog's body temperature is higher than ours, so they prefer water that is quite hot (at least mine do). I highly recommend the pre-bath training, suction cup leash, and hand-held nozzle.

Sidney Hardie

Going to School

Mr. Keeper and I are going out for our walk at the beach (this is to wear him out before we go to school, so he'll at least listen during class every now and then). We get to the park, and in his excitement to get out of the van, he knocks my glasses off. One lens falls out and the fishing line thing that holds it in place breaks. No big deal, except these are my spare glasses; my good glasses are already at the eye doctor's awaiting a new lens that someone chewed a week or so ago. So off we go on our walk, me half blind, Keeper ready to snap at those waves that just keep coming and coming. He's having a wonderful time, playing mountain goat up and down the broken cement along the shore. I step in a hole and twist my ankle. Next thing I know he's rummaging in a pile of leaves; no problem, until he comes back with a muskrat (already dead) and prances around with his tail going 1000 miles per hour. I'm yelling at him to drop it (yah, right). Finally he puts it down to get a better grip, and I get him away from it. Thankfully I didn't have to actually touch the thing! By now I'm ready to go home!

We are now at home and it's nearly time to go to school. I'd left everything in the van when we got home, so he didn't have his leash on-no problem as he'll drop anything to go for a ride. Anything that is except for the two small boys and their small dog that were walking up the street! He's out zooming around them. When Keeper is free, he bounces and spins much like a bucking bronco. I tell the boys that he just wants to play and he won't hurt them at all. Of course COME doesn't mean anything to him (why do you think we're going to school?); and every time I get close, he zooms just out of my reach. One of the little boys decides he will help catch the wild boy by CHASING him. You can already guess how successful that ploy was! We finally walk their dog up to my house, I open the back of the van, and in Keeper jumps, whew! I apologize to the boys, who were wonderful, seeing they had an 80 pound crazy dog running around.

If I hurry, I'll just be a couple minutes late for class, EXCEPT, Keeper has locked the van door. My keys are in the ignition and my purse with the spare key is locked in the car, too. I go in the house and call our instructor, explain I'll be a little late, and grab a screwdriver (thank goodness my dad put a spare key behind my license plate for just such occasions). Of course, Keeper was a snot at class, more interested in blades of grass than what anyone was telling him! Why didn't someone warn me of the Teddy Principle when I named him KEEPER????

Linda Cunningham

When you call Monty to come, he runs in to you and sometimes likes to bounce off you into the "sit in front" by jumping and placing a paw in your groin. In obedience matches, do you lose points for the recall if you end up lying on the ground writhing as waves of pain rush from your groin up your spine like some kind of sadistic Kundalini?

Marc Lawrence

If I had a quarter for every time Branagan didn't make it back to me on the recall when he was a youngster, I'd be able to retire! He visited every new dog, every new person, and anything interesting along the way! Same thing in agility-off lead-off to visit! He has such a loving, goofy personality that he made everyone laugh and got away with it because no one could be serious around him.

I really got a kick out of him in Ohio at the Hunting/Working weekend. Airedalers were coming up to me saying, "Wow, your 'Dales pay such close attention to you in the ring" (we work off lead, of course). I'm thinking, "When did that transition finally happen?" We worked so hard on it that when it finally gels (Hey, we're a TEAM here), and everything clicks, you're just happy it finally went right! I don't know if we'll ever win any titles, but we sure have fun and have met some great dogs and wonderful people. I only wish every dog club could be as understanding for every type of dog!

Yvonne Michalak

Thunderstorms

The Rescue Remedy is great stuff. I have used it twice during thunderstorms and Monty was calmer but also obviously felt like himself-unlike with tranquilizers which make him an 80 lb. blob and scare me half to death. During the first storm, I had some warning, gave him the RR and he was calmer; but I didn't have his crate ready for him to use, so it was only a partial test.

When another storm came up suddenly the other night, I gave Monty the Rescue Remedy, put his rug in his crate, put a blanket over the top of the crate, and put a few of his toys inside. He came downstairs, checked out the crate, walked in and out about 6 times, and then laid down in it. The crate had not been moved from its location, which was in my laundry room next to the clothes dryer which was going at the time. Perhaps the sound of the drum going at the same time helped drown out the thunder. He did moan for a few minutes and was quiet after that.

As soon as the storm passed, I took him outside, brought his Frisbee, his ball, played in the wet grass, etc. (The neighbors who know us think its funny; the rest of them think I am nuts.) As an extra added attraction, I took him for a 5 minute ride in the car, his favorite thing. I think the above included everyone's suggestions and they all worked. As far as dropping things to get him used to sudden noises, according my "better half" I do that anyway; and if Monty isn't used to it by now, he never will be. Anyway, I do try to get the pots/tops together (when Dad's at work) and make some noise. He does seem to be getting less startled by it.

Roe Quinn

I favor playing with my dogs vigorously while completely ignoring the passing storm. The idea is that they get too distracted to remember to be afraid. I have a theory that, to dogs, thunder sounds like the world's biggest dog growling at them. Dogs can learn to be blasé about all kinds of things through practice and experience.

Ken McE

Abby has a very strong hunting instinct that she must have been born with. She would fetch when very, very little and was constantly sniffing the ground when just a baby. But the biggest quirk she has is the love of loud noises! She becomes incredibly excited at the sound of a gun, or anything that even resembles a gun. She does the same thing when my husband just gets a gun out of the safe. Her mouth foams up, her ears prick up, her eyes just sparkle. She loves the hunt! There is a downside to this, though. She must be kept inside when we weed-eat the yard, as she tries to kill the weed-eater. The skill-saw elicits the same response. The worst and most dangerous was the nail gun. We just finished a remodel project and my husband had to be sure she was well confined before he used it. She is so intent on what she considers the prey, she pays no attention to life or limb. Silly dog! In this case, it's a good thing she's not depended upon to provide dinner for us. I'd never know what to serve with a skill-saw!

Shelly Treat

Press Button for Service

Believe me, this particular whining is not distress unless it is the distress of not having my attention when she wants it. She whines for the joy of whining. If the food or water bowls are OHMYGOD empty, Gussie barks; but she will lie on the kitchen floor and whine while wagging her tail. Human comes to investigate and the real cause is found-whining is reserved for demanding a FUZZYTUMMY RUB.

Stella is more direct-she walks up, bangs her head into whatever part of your body is nearby so as to get your attention, gives it a BIGFUZZYPAWSLAP and tries to communicate telepathically. Try to ignore her and you get a more insistent BIGFUZZY PAWSLAMDUNK and her head resting on you while demanding, "Look deeply into my big beautiful eyes" so she can properly hypnotize you and get that pig ear from the pantry that is calling her name. Meanwhile, if Gussie tries to interrupt Stella's routine, they'll end up sitting side-by-side looking like fighting walruses as they bang their heads and open mouths together (BITEFACE) or into the aforementioned human body part that might be in the way.

Morgan Kelley

My little Willow will be 6 months old on January 6th. She doesn't like having her ears examined. She reminds me of my children when they were young. You know darn well that it doesn't hurt, but they just have to complain anyway! Whether the pain is real or imagined, I swear Airedales do it for attention. Just yesterday I decided that I was going to go for my 3-4-5 mile walk solo. Willow was downstairs behind the babygate in the family room. Hubby had just walked up to see me off when all of a sudden we heard this blood-curdling scream from Willow. It sounded like she was caught in something and was in gut-wrenching pain. Hubby and daughter raced to her rescue. There she stood wagging her tail as if to say, "It worked!" She had simply wanted to go for a walk with her mommy. Hubby feeling sorry for her (loves her more than me), brought her to me and told me that I should take her with me. Have you ever tried to walk, I mean really walk, with a puppy at your side, straining to get to the ditch to tuckbuttrun through the snow or snag a stick? It turned out fine; however, it wasn't what I had planned. Oh, well. Time well spent with my best friend! But, Airedales ARE CRYBABIES!

Michelle Rolandson

Boarding

As a boarding kennel owner, maybe I can help you feel more comfortable. Call the kennel and make an appointment for a preliminary visit. I find the best visits are without the dog, and without a health record the dog cannot enter anyway. Make sure the kennel requires vaccinations. Ask about the cleaning procedure and feeding schedule. A recent magazine article said call the ABKA (American Boarding Kennel Association) for a referral. Well, this is an organization that you pay dues to belong to and doesn't necessarily mean that the members are good or bad kennels. I would rather see you ask people you know for recommendations.

Please don't take an old shirt, afghan, or anything that may have a hole in it. There is a chance that your dog could put a head or foot through the hole and twist during the night. This could be fatal. Bedding that I prefer to see people bring is a lambswool type dog rug, with no stuffing. This way, if the dog has an accident from nervousness, I can wash and hang it out to dry. Also make sure you remove all collars from the dog when you leave, for the same reason. Taking them with you is best. Don't take food and water bowls; a good kennel only uses stainless steel and they are disinfected each day. Toys are great but evaluate each one carefully and make sure there is no danger.

When you drop off your dog, sign a release for treatment, provide emergency numbers (where you'll be or that of a friend that you would like to be involved in your place). On my release form I have a special section for anything unusual I should know about your pet, for example: gets hot spots, sleeps a lot, has a cyst on stomach. This way I'll know to watch for the hot spots, sleeping a lot is normal, or the lump I felt is known to the owners and has been checked by a vet. Make your good-bye's to your dog short. The dog is most stressed when you stand outside and make it seem like it's going to be an awful experience. The dog does best when you make it seem fun and like he's going to camp for the week! You can take your own food or use the kennel's. Either way. I provide a good quality food and really don't find dogs having problems with switching (and you would be able to tell when cleaning). But if your dog is on a special diet or you prefer not to change, take your own.

Linda Klingerma

Growling

'My 9 month male, Trevor, my first 'dale, took a Kleenex and was eating it, a usual thing if he can do it. My daughter started to pry it out of his mouth and he growled at her. I stepped in and he growled at me, too, and showed his teeth."

Airedales will growl to try to establish that they are the Alpha, or to express displeasure, or to play, or to say, "I really don't want to do this right now." If you think you are being challenged, don't put up with it for a second. YOU are the alpha! Trevor needs a firm "NO!" and if necessary, a pop under the chin.

Our guys like to grab something and then let us try to get it away from them. It is a game. To a non-Airedale person, this could be worrisome. Geoffrey is a growler and sounds really scary to folks not familiar with 'dales. He has the teeth to scare the faint of heart. He also grumbles about lots of things, including our trying to pry something out of his mouth. Brady, by contrast, will clamp something in the Jaws of Death but won't make a sound! So, if you think you are being challenged for real, you need to establish yourself as the Alpha. If Trevor is playing a game you don't want to play, your response should be different. Communicate the message "not now," but not "bad dog."

Karl Broom

P.S. As soon as you think you understand Trevor's rules of the game, he will change the game!

In general, what should people do if their dog does growl at them?

A dog living in a house with people is still living in a pack. This is a young dog that does not know the pack hierarchy. At 9 months, he is like a teenage boy-just ready to test the world. He is testing the pack leader. If he thinks a pack leader has not been selected, he is designating himself as pack leader. Do not allow this.

When I sell new puppies to new owners, I make sure they know what to do when the pup tests them. I make sure all my pups allow me to take things away from them. On the other hand, I will play tug with the pups and let them win. My reasoning is that it builds up their confidence; but when I take things away from them, they still know I am boss. My dogs all go through the door before I do, they all go downstairs before I do, and if I feel so inclined, they eat before I do. But, they all know that I am the boss. Alpha bitch, you say??? You bet.

To help you with your growling pup (because he is still a baby, regardless of his size): if he has something he shouldn't have, treat him like a pack leader would treat him. Grab him firmly by the scruff of the neck (not the collar; you have better control with the scruff), hold him firmly, grab what he has and take it away. If you have a firm hold with one hand, he should not be able to grab your other hand. He may not even try. Don't let your daughter do this until the pup has learned that you are the boss. When that is established, then if he challenges her, you, in turn, challenge him.

Give him a situation to test him. During this, you must show no fear and be decisive with your actions. Give him something he likes, a bone or Kong or toy. Give it to him for a minute or so, then talk to him and reach to take it away. If he growls, grab him by the scruff quickly, take it away, admire it for a minute or so. Talk to it and to him -isn't this pretty? is it yours?-then give it back to him. Do not tease him with it. You are just proving a point here. You gave it to him in the first place, you can take it away from him, but he knows you may give it back (if it is not something he shouldn't have). Repeat the procedure. I do this with all my dogs, only I use beefy knuckle bones for a real test.

Ginny Higdon

Selective Deafness

One thing I have done lately to address the problem of an older dog ignoring my calls, and a younger one who had started to do the same, is use a clicker. I "loaded the clicker" for a couple of days -every time they started towards me at all, I clicked and they got liver, which they love because it smells strong. After a couple of days, I would be able to just go to the back door and click and it was amazing the group I would attract. So much nicer at night than my melodious tones screeching, which I have to confess, while recognizing its ineffectiveness, I did sometimes resort to out of frustration. The click is a very clear sharp sound and penetrates. Now, I have to admit my clicker and I still cannot compete with a mole in the woodpile!!

Ellen Cornell

Using a Crate

I never had a crate before I got Charlie but he came crate trained. In fact, he trained me so that I could train Nell. They give the animal security and help protect it when you have to be out.

I just recently put a rescue dog on a plane to Michigan. I'm not sure this guy had ever been around a crate and I wondered what I was going to do about getting him to ride in one at the airport. I had given him some food in it the night before. He crawled in it voluntarily when I was taping the papers to the top and slept in it without a peep. This guy had been through a lot and when I walked him into the airport and he saw his crate waiting with his blanket in it, he dove right in. It really helped him on the trip. I will never have another dog that is not crate-trained.

Mary Giese

Do you know that you can fit two small children and a 20 lb. puppy nicely into a Vari 400? I have the cutest picture of my two godchildren and Brodie inside Brodie's crate. The first time the boys came over to see Brodie, they thought it was the most amazing thing that he had his own house and they just had to investigate. "Do you think Brodie will let us go in his crate?" Not only did he let them, he also climbed right in and proceeded to cover the two of them with puppy BIGWETKISSES! Too funny!

Diane Maxwell

Surf Training

When Toby was one and I took the list's advice of placing mouse traps on the counters under sheets of paper to scare him off counter surfing, I came home and found only the metal snaps of the traps remaining. Apparently he'd eaten the wooden parts. Toby still occasionally tries to counter surf at home, but I am so dog-trained that nothing is within his reach.

Unfortunately my parents are not so well trained. When they kept Toby last week while my other dog was recovering from cataract surgery, Toby grabbed a doughnut from an end table after my mother had cut it in half to eat it, and later he got a piece of hot pizza off the counter! I was there for the pizza incident. Toby doesn't like to be yelled at it and it was something to see him cowering on the floor with cheese and pepperoni dripping out of his mouth. I got it before he could swallow it.

Mary Jane Smetanka

Gitte Koopmans' anti-surfing trick which worked for her Targa and Sherry's Keeper (littermates): put pennies or pebbles into two empty soda cans and tape the openings. Attach either end of a piece of string to each can and tie a really good, stinky treat such as a cheese or hot dog cube in the middle. Set the cans slightly back on the counter with the treat easily accessible at the edge. Hide and let the culprit approach to steal the treat.

When the dog takes the treat, the cans will clatter to the floor, and the dog will be startled-if she is of a temperament to be startled. You need to dart in quickly enough to grab the treat before the dog recovers and eats it. If the dog eats the treat, her surfing adventure will be self-reinforcing despite the scary noise.

Sherry Rind

Using Treats

The terrier needs a reason to obey until that time when it is habit or just feels right to them. One of my males was sneaking into a pen where a female was in heat. He knew that he wasn't supposed to be there and normally if he is spoken to sharply, he comes back the way he went out. But this time he was playing stupid with that "duh" look. This went on perhaps 5 times. I was watching for him and caught him going through a small space around the gate (so small I wouldn't have believed it if I hadn't seen it). I stepped out the door, said his name sharply and he hung his head as if to say "auhhhh *%#$@, I got caught." He came back through where he went out and half way back to me I could see a light go on in his head that said "safe place here I come." He took a couple of hops and was in heel position looking at my face as if he trusted completely that this was the correct choice. I of course cracked up! And he was correct.

I use treat rewards and have for the first time come up against a dog that doesn't have much of a food drive. I am astounded at how much harder the training is. Guess that is the reason I believe that breeders must understand what they are breeding and the true short-coming in the dogs that they have or are considering breeding to. Having a pronounced food drive makes things so very much easier.

I think Airedales must, at least in the beginning, have a reason to work. One of the puppies from my last litter went to a home where the owner was using small pieces of the pup's regular food for the beginning training. Not surprisingly he had no success, then he was tuned into using bits of meat and was surprised at the happiness that his puppy displayed when "working." Another puppy went to a home where the dog before had been a "heeler." The man also tried to teach without a good reason and said that sometimes the pup was into it and sometimes not. Then he bought a leg of lamb and trimmed the fat off. He called me to tell me how quickly that puppy got a fast sit, what focus that he had, and ever since then he was still fast even if there was no treat. I told him no doubt the pup thought that the boss had finally learned. He is now using "good reasons" for his dog to obey. In time the things that you are doing with the dog become the only correct thing the dog wants to do.

No matter what the dog is willing to work for -a ball or what ever he has told you-you require more and more from him until he will work with a promise of it later. This same puppy became a good retriever. The puppy came to the owner with a stick and it was thrown at 2 o'clock twice. He came back with it both times. The next time it was at 11 o'clock but the puppy wasn't watching where it was thrown, just that it went. He again went to 2 o'clock-no stick-back to dad, look at him, is this a trick?, back to 2 o'clock, back to dad. Then out to look and use his nose to find that stick and return it to dad very pleased with himself! During this time dad was quiet and still; he just let the puppy work it out on his own. I am sure that he was amazed and that is why I heard about it. I think the reason that this puppy would work through a problem such as this is that he was being trained; he wanted to please, and he used his brain.

Terry Brunner

Training the Human

Yesterday I discovered that Charlie, my big boy, has been extorting biscuits from both the mailman and my neighbor's 12 year old step-son. He apparently barks until they hand over the goodies. I never would have known without seeing the mailman "perform" on com-mand and hearing the boy's confession ("I've been feeding Charlie biscuits through the fence and he lets me pet him now.")
Charlie has the mailman trained so that if he comes up to the mail-box outside the fence without the goodies, Charlie barks loudly, jumps wildly and sticks his face and neck through the fence. This sends the mailman back to the truck for said biscuits which he gives to Charlie, eliciting the friendly tail wag. Oh, that dog!

Mary Giese

About 5:50 a.m. this morning, I was rudely awakened by Bonnie barking at us from the foot of the bed. I mumbled something about being quiet and pulled the covers up tighter. Well, Bonnie is nothing if not persistent: I heard more barking. Then Beau chimed in and began barking at us, too. I thought if I just ignore them, maybe Roy will get up. I then asked "Do you have to go potty?" Of course that was met with more riotous barking and then pouncing on the bed. Finally my husband got up to let them out. I was immediately drifting off to sleep again when I heard "Moooouoooo" and "Groooaaannn" and more mooing from the foot of the bed. I asked "Who's there?" Bonnie came around to the side of the bed and stuck her wet nose in my face. My husband was by now walking back into our room and climbing back into bed. Beau was bounding back into the room, too. Roy said to me, "You're gonna have to get up to let Bonnie out; she won't go with me." As soon as I sat up, I could hear Bonnie doing a little geriatric HAPPYDANCE as she watched me put on my slippers. She was very pleased with herself as I got up and walked with her down the hall to let her out back to go potty. Now, may I ask, "Who's trained?" I wonder why she thinks I'm the only one qualified to let her outside? Could it be that she thinks Dad doesn't know that she always has a biscuit when she comes in from her morning potty time? Is she totally stuck in a rut? Beau doesn't take time to worry; he just goes with whoever opens the door. I know she loves my husband and enjoys his petting her but she believes I'm the one who's supposed to take care of her needs and she makes certain that I stay in line. She's the BOSS!

Judy Dwiggins

Advanced Class

Maddog and I are two weeks away from our third attempt to pass advanced class. (Here in Australia it goes: beginners, intermediate, advanced, novice offlead, and open.) Mad is a reasonable heeler and a great stayer. The problem comes with a down command during a heeling pattern. She will do two or so, then if required to do more, will completely refuse! She gets that "oh Mum, why do I have to do it again" look. She is a "soft" dog and no amount of coaxing, food, or sharp command will make this dog drop at the required time.

Our second problem is recall. Here we are required to have a cord line attached, give a stay command and walk six meters away and call the dog. Mad stays, and stays and doesn't come. I'm despondent about this as she knows how to do these and will do them, although inconsistently. We practice regularly and the thought of failing again makes me wonder where the point is to all this. We do enjoy class and got this far with no repeats. Any suggestions?

Toni Mcinnes

Well, of course! She's done it twice already (and probably did it right) so there isn't any point to doing it again. One of the hardest things for an Airedale trainer to get through is the intelligence of this breed-you can't repeat things ad nauseum like you would do for a golden retriever or one of the herding breeds.

It's hard to diagnose obedience problems from halfway around the world, but I'll give it a try. My guess is that you haven't gotten Mad switched over to a schedule of variable reinforcement, which you just about have to do to be able to have success in the harder obedience work. (I'm not very good at it, so I'm an expert!) When you are practicing all of your obedience work, you need to stop rewarding every successful performance and start first by rewarding maybe every other one, then every third one, then try and switch yourself to a schedule where you reward sometimes the first one, sometimes the 4th or 5th, sometimes the second. Variable reinforcement is THE MOST IMPORTANT TOOL YOU'VE GOT for creating consistent performance. I know it sounds backwards, but it isn't. Think of gamblers-why do people get addicted? It's certainly not because they win every time. What you'll discover is that Mad will work harder and harder to get that reward!

Barbara Mann

The Walkdown

Fergie finally gave me the opportunity I have been waiting for to get a beginning handle on her "run away" behavior. (But why do these dogs always wait for the most inopportune times to do this sort of stuff-it was COLD out there!) I was getting ready to take the trash out to the curb and wanted all dogs in the house so I could open gates and leave them open without having escapees. Fergie caught on to the fact that I was doing something that she would rather be outdoors for and proceeded to dance away from me. So I did what I have preached to others-I called her exactly once and then proceeded to "walk her down." Briefly, this means I wouldn't play the chase game that she clearly wanted me to play, but just plodded after her without saying a word and without getting excited. (I sure was glad I had already put on my jacket, hat, and gloves! The high today was about 10 degrees F and it was dropping at the time I did this.)

At first she would wait until I was fairly close and then tear off, wagging her tail and expecting me to start screaming at her and chase her. But I didn't-surprise, surprise. After a while, she started dancing around me just out of reach. So I stood perfectly still and ignored her until she took off again. Then-plod, plod, plod. After about 10 minutes of this (all inside the fenced yard, by the way), she finally came in very close to me and stopped. I told her to sit. She did. I got a hand on her collar and told her what a good girl she was, hooked her up on the leash I had grabbed during one of our laps around the yard, and took her into the house. HA! That didn't work out quite like you expected, did it, Miss Fergie? You could see the wheels turning in her smart little head, so I hope this made an impression.

It was much easier doing this routine with her than it was with Barney, the dog I had to learn it for. With Fergie, I had the experience of knowing that it works. With Barney, I was just following directions that I had been given by an experienced trainer. And Barney almost out-lasted me: our first walk down took 30 minutes!

Barbara Mann

Communication

My ADT, Ben, talks to me with growls. When he first started doing it, I thought it was possibly aggression but it wasn't. I started to listen to his growls and tried to make an association with each growl. I know when he's hungry, thirsty, needs to go out, wants to play, wants attention, wants a special toy that he can't find, "don't bother me I'm sleeping," etc. Sometimes the growls become barks which really mean that there is an urgency. Ben is always friendly with people-both those he knows and those he's meeting for the first time. The only time I became concerned was when he decided he had had it with his groomer. I knew it was coming because his groomer was being aggressive and verbally abusive to him. A little sweet talk from me and some gentle rubs calmed the situation, cleared the air, and created a truce between the groomer and Ben. Let's say Ben made his point then, too.

Arlene Black

Dalton talks with growls, too! He has different growls and they are different from aggression growls. He uses them a lot with me and my youngest daughter because we are his favorites. My in-laws used to think he was really growling at my daughter; but now that they know him and have seen him talk that way, they know it is different, too. It is pretty neat! He has a really neat relationship with my youngest, who is four.

Vicki Mitchell

Merlin is usually very vocal when we are on the agility course-either one of us starts the conversation. Either I ask him a question and get a growl-talk response or he growl-talks something to me and I respond. In either case the conversation can go on for quite a while. At one time, there was a speech pathologist or therapist in one of our classes. She listened to him for several weeks and then started talking back to him IN GROWL TALK. And he tilted his head to one side, came to full attention and ANSWERED HER. I have a pretty good ear for "furry-ign" languages, but hers was much better. She said that he was repeating many of the same morphemes and/or phonemes in repeated, recognizable sequences which were mixed in other sequences. She said that with training he and I might be able actually to communicate [C'mon Dad, I'm communicating wif u now-U just aren't listening.] effectively.

Bill Austin

Teaching "No Bark"

You may recall my story of Charlie's barking problem this past weekend. Well when Roe talked of Montgomery being taught not to bark, I embarked literally on the BARK. I thought there may have been a slight communication problem between my little ADT imp, Charlie, and myself so I got right down and barked. Now my bark wasn't as tough as his but it would pass for an Airedale bark I am sure. Charlie's first response was a strange little Airedale tilt of the head when I said "NO BARK" then I barked and said "NO BARK." He looked puzzled but he responds now to "NO BARK." So when he runs out to bark out the neighbor dogs I merely say, "NO BARK, Charlie." He looks at me as if to ask "Why not?" and then silently watches what the other dogs are doing. Hooray for the NO BARK lesson. I really think he is just humoring me because he thinks I have really gone off the deep end with this bark business.

Bobbi Sparr

Charlie must be a smart little cookie to catch on that quickly. It is amazing; that's exactly what Monty did when I worked with him on the same problem. The tilt of the head, but he did recognize the two words/sounds together. He rarely snarls but when he starts to growl at anything or anybody he gets one sharp "Quiet" and that usually ends that.

Now Monty knows enough not to break into an all-out barking spree unless absolutely necessary. The other night (about 11:30), he began to carry on something awful, insisting I get off the computer and come upstairs. Sure enough, I opened my front door (the full glass storm door was locked) and saw a few young men who had wandered away from a party around the corner. They obviously had decided to try to walk it off and it must have been proving more difficult than expected. Well, one of them decided to sit on the curb in front of my house and put his head on his knees. His 3 buddies were trying to convince him that he was fine but he wasn't. Then Monty let go and I don't think I ever saw such a quick recovery. He was scrambling to his feet, moving at a good pace practically on all fours, and yelling back, "It's okay, I'm fine, I'm leaving! Please, lady, don't let your dog out!" Well, we know Monty would have probably licked them to death but they didn't know that.

Roe Quinn

In the yard Rusty barks at birds and the neighborhood dogs, the deer, the elk. Pretty much everything. It's not so bad because there's usually some distance between my ears and his mouth. It's when he's in the car that it becomes annoying. He'll bark at horses, big trucks, motorcycles, other dogs walking along the street; you never know when the urge will strike him to belt out a big, brain-scrambling, Airedale, basso profundo bark. I tried squirting him with water. He opened his mouth for a drink. I tried holding his leash and yanking, etc. It got to be dangerous to drive with Rusty because I was always trying to correct him for barking. Out of desperation, I tried yelling NO! at the top of my lungs. It worked! He barks and I yell. What a pair. He is now eking out little, whinny "woofs" as opposed to "WOOF." I'm still yelling and it's working. Hopefully we will have him cured before I lose my voice permanently. We drive with the windows up and the AC on so as not to seem too wacko.

David Weaver

I let Mr. Charles out today and lickety split he went BARK BARK BARK. I went to call him into the house. Then we had a little lecture about the pros and cons for his little ADT life for frivolous BARKING in this neighborhood. I reinforced with the fact that NO BARK gets a chewie. I thought about this little conversation I had and thought to myself, "If he understands all that human gibberish, he is one VERY INTELLIGENT dog." Guess what? Not a peep since the lecture.

He is too much.

Bobbi Sparr

Introducing a New Dog

"This is where I need some advice from all you adopters, rescuers, breeders, and multi-dale syndrome inflicted listers. Other than a health check, what things should I look into? What should I look for in Indy-Cleo interactions that would indicate a suitable match? How long should I really take to evaluate the situation? How do young 'dales react when an older 'dale is brought into the picture? Would an older female/younger male factor play into this?"

Richard Blackwell

They will let you know very quickly if they are compatible. I agree that you should introduce them on neutral territory and bring them home and into the home situation together. They will probably play very hard and then lie down next to each other to recuperate. You may have a squabble or two and they will sound awful, like they are killing each other, but if there is no blood, don't let it panic you. Three or four of mine do it every time they go out the door. Visitors usually get upset. If it were serious, believe me, there would be blood.

Jack McLaughlin

Training Multiple Dogs

Sherry was asking how people manage to clicker train multiple dogs. This question just came up on one of the clickerlists and Debi Davis, a wonderful person who trains Papillons to be her service dogs, explained how she does it. She gave me permission to pass it along to the Airedale list:

To start, I'll share how I manage multiples in my household. First, I no longer isolate the other dogs and work with one dog separately, unless it's a very new behavior I'm just introducing, and need as distraction-free environment as possible. What I found was that the isolated dogs stressed way too much, and when their turn came, they over-compensated, in manic fashion. What I do instead is click all the dogs at the same time at first, for a collective behavior. It might be sits, downs or doggie pushups. Just something simple all the dogs can do in a line in front of me, at the same time. One click nets a reinforcer for each dog. I then single out one dog and have that dog do a sit or down. I cue the other dogs to another part of the room and put them in a down stay. The dog I'm working with then gets to work on a separate behavior while the others watch. Each time I click the dog I'm working with, I give the other dogs a verbal "keep going" signal and toss them a tiny, tiny treat. This reinforces that being left out of the one-on-one is still rewarding, and that though I am not working with them at the moment, I am still noting their excellent behaviors and reinforcing them.

Meanwhile, I am working with the selected dog on targeting, on retrievals, on opening and shutting doors or pressing a button. If I am doing rapid reinforcements, I try to remember to stop and reinforce the other dogs for remaining quiet every 5 clicks or so. I do this because it's very, very hard for these dogs not to whine and stress when they don't get their chance to be clicked. It just sets them up for success and allows me the space to do individual shaping. With a puppy, I cannot expect these quiet behaviors for a long enough time, so I have an x-pen set up in my living room. I pop the pup in the pen, and watch from my peripheral vision. Again, I keep verbally marking his quiet behaviors inside the pen and tossing him tiny treats. This keeps the puppy from whining.

I also do "round robin" training with them all together. I may have one dog in front of me, practicing opening and shutting a door. I'll have the other dogs to my left or right, practicing placement exercises, and again, with each click, each dog gets reinforced for something. I practice ringing the doorbell, and moving through the door separately, but in a line. One dog rings bell, goes outside, gets clicked and tossed a treat. The other dogs do not get reinforced except with a verbal "goood." The next dog in line gets to do the behavior, and then waits outside after his tossed treat. When the last dog gets through the door, we turn around and reverse the process, ringing the bell to go INSIDE, one by one.

Debi Davis Tucson, AZ

Unlocking The JAWS OF DEATH

Someone call the ASPCA on me. Laddie went too far and I had to clobber him. Laddie loves picking trash up on his walks and walking with it until I wrestle it off of him or he gulps it down. The other night he walked with a cup in his mouth actually covering his nose until we got home (that was amusing). A few "drop its" and actually taking it away did the trick. That was the easy one. The hard one was a piece of bread or something. I had to almost pick him up with the choke chain and grab it with the other. It's a challenge and very frustrating when I can't get the trash in time and end up in the Vet's office after hours.

Today he went too far and so did I. He picked up a dead pigeon by the side of the road; I yelled for him to drop it and of course he clamped down and wouldn't let go. It freaked me out with its legs sticking out of his mouth. I kept a tight hold on him with the choke chain because he was trying to run with it so he could eat it. I couldn't let him do that; I was remembering a litter of puppies that died of coccydiomycosis (or the disease transmitted by bird feces). No matter how much I choked him with the choker, he wasn't dropping so I had to inflict pain on him; but that didn't work. I guess it did because he dropped it at one point when I was going to smack him again-all on the butt area, of course, but this dog feels no pain and I just don't know what to do short of mistreating him when he does something like this. The ear pinching I was advised to try doesn't work at all. I could drill a hole through his ear flap and he'll whine but swallow the thing whole. Even the gum pinching with the teeth doesn't work; I've had men do it with all their strength and he holds on and won't let go.

I'm especially ticked today because if it had been something else and he had swallowed it, I could have lived with that, (like the time he swallowed a dead rotten fish whole) but I had to actually hurt him because he's so stubborn. Stubborn is not even the word: it's his way or no way. I'm ticked at myself for having to hurt him and still he wouldn't let go. I wish there was an easier way. If anybody else has any suggestions, please let me know.

Loly Nieves

Why don't you try a trade program. Bring along some treat that he really loves, like cheese cubes or hot dog slices. Set him up by placing something on the sidewalk you know he'll take. When he does, offer him a treat as a trade for the object. As soon as he drops the object and heads for the treat "click" with a clicker to reinforce his behavior and give him the treat. Slowly work a hand cue and then a verbal along with a hand cue into the schedule until he performs flawlessly. One note: don't start with dead birds. Use something less alluring but still tempting as a starting point and slowly move up to the point where he will reject dead birds as well.

If he doesn't comply simply mark the instance with a "no reward mark" and up the anti on the treats. I don't know too many Dales who wouldn't trade a paper towel for a piece of cheese. There are some good books on this subject. Check out Don't Shoot the Dog by Karen Pryor and The Culture Clash by Jean Donaldson.

Mike Marzo

Toggle has the same propensity; but when I got him, he had been trained with the commands "leave it" and "drop it." "Leave it" also works when he has something in his mouth as well as when he is just trying to go after something that I don't want him to, such as a cat when we're walking. Perhaps others who have done more training than I could give better instructions but the key is to get the behavior trained when you control the environment, i.e. at home.

When Toggle picks up a piece of Kleenex or discarded food or dead thing, I can say "drop it" and he will if he is on the leash. I walk him with a prong collar, and a quick tug and release if he does not follow the command immediately will get him to do it. Now he knows that is what will happen, so I rarely have to follow through. My guess is that you teach him initially by saying "drop it," having him drop the toy and rewarding him. Practice about 10 minutes twice each day if you can fit it in. The more you practice, the quicker he'll generalize it. Start with least favored toys and move up to his favorite toys, then fast food wrappers, wrappers with fast food still in them, etc., all on your turf. To bolster you on walks, you may take a favorite treat, something that he rarely gets but loves. With my first Airedale, it was cheese. She just adored it and would drop most things for cheese. You can use a good treat on your walks to reward him when he drops the icky thing. Especially initially when he is learning the behavior. Eventually, you should be able to fade out the food reward and just give the command; or if you use a clicker, use that instead. It may take awhile because his current habit is pretty deeply entrenched behavior and highly self-rewarding.

Mary Giese

Boy, can I empathize with you, Loly! Fergie, for all that she is a veritable tidbit of an Airedale, has the strongest darn jaw muscles of any dog I've ever dealt with and she doesn't want to let go of a treasure for anything! I came home from dog training club Wednesday night in the first stages of flu and threw my jeans into the laundry basket without doing a careful pocket check to make sure I had gotten out all the training treats. The next morning, when I was really sick, Ferg discovered that there were some dried up hot dogs in one of the pockets and was in the process of tearing through the pocket material to get them out. I had a devil of a time prying her loose and was thoroughly pissed off by the time I retrieved the jeans. I won't tell you what abuse I dealt out to her in the process.

When I get a dog as a puppy, I teach "leave it" from a very early age, but nobody taught this to Fergie. [Note: read about Fergie in the Rescue chapter.] Next best thing is "give." I've been starting her on it with a toy. She loves to chase and retrieve stuffed toys but doesn't like to give them to me-she'd rather play tug of war. Since she is a very dominant dog who has had biting problems, I INSIST on her releasing it to me. I tell her "give" ONCE, then I pry it loose. As soon as it is out of her jaws, she gets praise and a pat and I throw it again. She's gotten much better about giving it up. She's not stupid-she caught on quickly that it was more fun to have me praise her and throw it again than to dance around waiting for me to chase her, a game I refuse to play. I won't chase and I won't play tug of war, but I'm happy to throw the thing for her for quite a while. (I also NEVER let her be the one who has the toy last. I always win.)

I've been thinking about what the next step will be in this training. I would like to work up to being able to get her to give me anything that she has in her mouth. The trick is to work on this in small steps, using things where the reward for giving it up is more desirable than the joy of having the object in her mouth. You might try something like this with Laddie. The time to train is not when he has the dead pigeon in his mouth, but while you are very firmly in charge of the situation and can control what happens.

Barbara Mann

Today, Rita got a bar of soap from John's gym bag, so of course he hollered at me to come take it away from her. Still dressed for church, I went to the living room and tried the "drop it" routine, in all of its variations. The fingers pushing the gums in on the teeth accomplished nothing but her attempting to draw the soap further back into her gullet. I ended up doing a very quick, forceful Dominant Down move with her, and even straddled her in my dress (Felt like Calamity Jane tying up a particularly obstinate heifer). This, incidentally, did not work. While I had her down, I used a bone to try and crowbar her jaws open. If I'd had an extra hand and a spoon it would have worked-could have shoved the soap forward and gotten it out at that point. No such luck. Finally, I let her back up and tried gravity, held her head down and worked on keeping her jaws slightly slack. She finally heaved it up (I think the dissolving soap was not tasting REAL good to her at that point) and I held her while John picked up the slimy, much smaller now, morsel of soap. Rita immediately relaxed and wanted me to pet her.

Is this whole routine a game? At least we were in the privacy of our own home, and I remembered that striking her would accomplish nothing except to vent my own anger. Observers may not realize the full implications of our Dales swallowing found objects. After reading some of your replies, I did want to offer empathy-I know what it's like to have one for whom NO treat is as alluring as whatever game seems to be going on. In the past, when I have had great success getting Rita to drop something and praised her heartily, her response has usually been to go and get something else so that we could do the whole routine again!

Gena Welch

I can relate to this topic. Indiana won't trade his finds easily; the command of give only works if he wants you to have it. I have resorted to a small spray bottle filled with water. I try and get the object from him. When I see it's not something he wants to give up, I spray him in the face, tell him "give" while I dig it out, and then reward. The spray seems to shock him enough that his mind goes to that instead of jaws of steel. Now we have days that I just show him the bottle and he changes his mind.

Mary Anne Pokorny

I got so much good advice and I thank you all. One thing I know is that Laddie will not give up a dead animal for a juicy steak. "Drop it" to him it means "Swallow it faster." Don't worry; Laddie wasn't hurt when he got his butt smacked; I was hurt emotionally having to do it. He finally let go because the bird was stuffed in his mouth so far he couldn't breathe. The only thing sticking out of his mouth were the legs of a full grown pigeon.

I decided to walk him with a muzzle. I know my Laddie and he is not compliant at all. I'm also going to try the spray bottle, although I've tried it with the hose and he'll just pick up the hose and run with it. That's my boy.

Loly Nieves

"I found the toe of the sock hanging out of his mouth & after a struggle managed to get the sock(minus some that was obviously predigested) out fromdown his throat. Do these dogs not have an active gag reflex?" Tania Joyce

I don't think they do! One time Sadie (RIP@RB) managed to untie a rawhide chew bone and swallow it whole. I just happened to look out into the backyard and notice her bopping around a little stranger than usual. I went out and just the slimy tip was sticking out between her teeth. I grabbed it and slowly pulled out about 18" of rawhide bone. After it was out, she wanted it back! What a gal.

Denise Duvall

Teddy does not pick trash up on her walks normally, but she would if someone else does. Last year, I took care of a puppy cocker spaniel. The pup was into trash on the street, so she'd pick up things like paper napkins and newspapers from right and left-we live in the city, so there is abundance of trash. What was funny was that as soon as the pup put the trash in her mouth, Teddy would take it right out of her mouth with the speed of light and spit it out the other way! The pup would constantly pick something up from the street and Teddy would diligently take it out of the pup's mouth right away. Knowing my Teddy, I know that she was just taking what she thought was potential goodies away from the pup for herself and only spat them out after realizing they were trash. But it sure looked like she was a mother who was disciplining her puppy! Really cute.

Kanako Ohara

For anyone who desperately needs to get an object out of a dogs mouth, and nothing seems to work, THIS WORKS! There is a small area right behind the rib cage on the dog's side that is extremely sensitive. If you press into this area with your fingers, the dog will immediately drop the object. I'm not sure why it works, but it does! My husband has had this demonstrated to him, and has used it successfully when our Winston was clamped onto a raccoon cage with THE JAWS OF DEATH and had no intention of ever letting go. A poke behind the rib cage did the trick, and saved his teeth!

Sandi Cooley

Dogs Must Be on Leash

Dear, departed Barley loved to carry the end of his leash when it was attached to him. Whenever I'd put the leash on to go anywhere, I could drop my end and he'd pick it up in the middle so he could hold it off the ground and keep it out of his way. Some of my fondest memories of him are of this happy, prancing Airedale walking himself to wherever we were headed. Near the end of his life, when visits to the vet were overly common, I would always let him walk himself into the vet's office. The office staff adored him and always laughed when they saw him coming. The sign on the wall read, "All animals must be on leash," but Barley and I knew that it didn't say a human being had to be holding the other end.

Barbara Mann

CHAPTER NINE

Airedale Rescue

FEW OTHER BREED rescues are as quick-acting, vehement, and passionate as Airedale Rescue groups. We do not love only our Airedales, but all Airedales; and we show it by taking action. Rescue never asks how much any particular dog is worth, nor does it judge the poorly conformed, puppy-mill ADT against the carefully bred show dog, the young against the old, the eager-to-please against the unsocialized. Some dogs come into Rescue well cared for and let go of reluctantly due to circumstances. Others are stinking, matted in mud and filth, and infected with heartworm; yet under the tangled fur will be seen the characteristic gleam in the eye, the ADT grin. Rescue need not judge because each dog is worth the effort. In addition to individual efforts, members of Airedale-L showed they have powerful group clout when Mary Gade appealed to the list as a last resort to rescue Piper as she was about to be put down. The response was instant, surprising to everyone but ourselves, and highly effective. Although Piper now lives happily with a family, she will always belong to the list because we became part of her life. This chapter contains her story, along with the stories of several others.

Few rescues are as challenging as Mary Giese's three. That hers was the best home for them becomes clear in the story of their rehabilitation, heavily condensed here from her web site. For full details, visit her web site at ww.geocities.com/Heartland/1364paradegiese.html.

My three ADTs are rescues Charlie, Nell and Toggle. Nell was rescued from a Minnesota collector farm with 400 dogs in pens on it. She was completely unsocialized and terrified of humans. She weighed 37 pounds and her undocked tail was bald. I brought her home in the car and that night when I took her out before bed, she slipped her collar and disappeared. I searched for her over the course of months. I got calls on sightings but no luck recapturing her. She avoided humans at all costs, but person after person kept telling me that she was making friends with their dogs, who would then let her eat out of their bowls.

Meanwhile, Charlie, a 75-pound handful, had been rescued from a pet shop when he was extremely ill. He was adopted by a family who returned him after he went after their housekeeper and threatened the teen-aged daughter's boyfriend. He was passed up by another rescue person because of his temperament and was languishing away at a boarding facility. I said I'd take him and ATRA agreed because there were no other options for him.

Five days after I got Charlie, the Humane Society called to say that they had captured Nell in a live trap. She had been gone for three months. She was as terrified of humans as ever but no fearbiter. The good news was that out on her own, she had proved to be quite the enterprising dog, gaining almost 30 pounds so she was at a normal weight of 65 pounds.

The first month I had them both was h*ll. Nell was terrified of me, terrified of Charlie, who tried to attack her every time she got close to me, and even terrified of the cat. The worst part was that she could hold her urine and feces for up to two days. I would take her out a dozen times a day and she would not go on the leash. I could not let her out unleashed because she'd try to escape. I had to keep a potty chart because I was afraid she'd burst. It is the first time that I have ever been grateful when a dog had an accident in the house.

She quickly housebroke herself, though, and I trained her to take food from my hand over the next month (my former special educator skills came in handy). In a couple of months, I was able to take her for walks off the leash by the river using treats to get her to come to me. She was still dealing with Charlie, who would periodically attack her. Our turning point with Charlie came when I strongly corrected him after he attacked her, and rather than running away, she watched. You could see the light bulb go on when she realized that I was dominant over him. After that she got braver around him and interacted more. She taught him to play rather than fight. And when we went out to the woods, she taught him how to hunt critters, i.e., chase madly after them.

The first several months I had Nell, she completely excavated my yard. Charlie, who was so meticulous he refused to drink from mud puddles and insisted I vacuum his crate whenever he saw dirt in it, was appalled. Now she has taught him to dig. Although she has pretty well given it up, he recently appears to be majoring in archeology. And she was the sneak thief. One time I came home after dark and woke up the next morning to find the following in my yard: my gym shorts, gym bra, one sneaker, one slipper, a food processor bowl and blade with the plastic piece chewed, an assortment of silverware and a toilet paper roll, unraveled as though the yard had been TP'd. It looked as if there had been a garage sale in my absence and, for all I know, there could have been.

I'd had them both for a year and a half when I decided maybe I was ready for a new challenge. There was this little guy named Toggle who growled and bit people. He is a perfect specimen from Canada and a long line of champions. He was trained with a heavy hand, however, and his owners gave him up when he did not fit their lifestyle. He had been in five homes since Memorial Day and, despite training, was too much for people to handle.

I flew to Michigan to pick him up. During one of our training sessions I made the mistake of trying to pat his head and he snapped at me, breaking my bracelet rather than my skin. (Rumor has it that he took off the thumbnail of one prospective owner, who quickly abandoned the idea of taking him.) My solution was to buy a pair of leather garden gloves on the way to the airport to take him home.

I spent the first week I had him wearing gloves to handle him so I wouldn't get bitten. I had to use time-outs for the growling because I did not want to put him through any physical correction. The time-outs worked and he quickly reduced his growling. Now, when he growls at me, he knows he has done something wrong and hangs his little head. He willingly goes to time-out for this, although I am beginning to add some different corrections. I spent a lot of time (and still do) hugging and touching him, which he has learned to like. He now comes up for hugs and kisses.

I waited two weeks before introducing him to Charlie, although he and Nell hit it off from the start. He challenged Charlie for dominance and lost. He and Charlie fought several times the first few days but pretty much worked it out. Charlie gets corrected and crated for other-dog aggression, which has helped. He typically gets along well with other dogs, however.

Toggle continues to need work on his people skills. He finds people very threatening and all new people get introduced slowly. My experience with the others tells me that I will probably need another year before I see major breakthroughs in this area. We continue to work on it.

Mary Giese

After hearing about an Airedale puppy in a pet store, Michael Jones sent the store manager the following letter. He invites others to use it as a model if they find ADTs in stores.

Dear Manager:

After a friend let me know that you have an Airedale puppy for sale in your store, my wife and I came by to look at and spend a little time with him. We currently have 2 Airedale Terriers as members of our family, and are concerned about the future of this puppy. Airedales are generally larger that the AKC standard calls for; our female is over 50 lbs., and our male is just over 60 lbs. and stands 26 inches at the withers. (They are very lean dogs that run agility.) It is not uncommon to see them at 75 to 80 lbs. The Airedale, like a lot of the Terriers, can be very headstrong, mischievous, and require a lot of patience to control. Add to this their size and strength and they become a formidable dog that without proper training and control could become destructive, if not dangerous. A common use of this dog is hunting of wild boar and bear, and in western states, mountain lions.

I did not get the feeling that your sales force had a clear understanding of the ultimate size and temperament of the Airedale. Many books recommend the breed to experienced owners only-not a good choice for someone to pick because it is cute as a puppy. While I would prefer that puppies not be sold at pet stores, the reason for my writing is to ask you to give my name and phone number to the purchasers of the Airedale puppy, not for the purpose of interfering with the sale, but to help with any training and questions about the breed. It is so easy to fall in love with a puppy, but not necessarily easy to live with long term. We are members of The Dog Training Club of St. Petersburg, and would like to help make sure that the puppy and its new owners have every chance to have a wonderful relationship. We also have contacts with the Airedale Rescue group for placing Airedales that are in need of a new home. I hope that this letter will be received in the spirit with which in was intended. We love our dogs and the breed, but they are a breed that requires special attention.

I would also ask if we could leave some information about the Dog Training Club Of St. Petersburg for distribution to your customers. The Club offers puppy, basic and advanced classes in obedience and agility for all dogs; mixed breeds are welcome. Our goal is to help people enjoy their pets. If I can be of any assistance, please contact me.

Michael Jones

My first Airedale was a sweet young lady who had lost her way in Petaluma. She'd been picked up by a man who just put her out in his backyard with about a dozen other strays. He'd feed them, but that was about it. When she came to me, I named her Aberdeen. Abby, as she was lovingly known to all of her new friends, absolutely loved baths. I'd ask her if she wanted to take a bath and off she'd go to the bathroom. She'd climb into the tub and wait for me. She was the best advertisement for Airedale rescue I could possibly imagine.

Now, if Miss Clementine hears the word bath, or senses that this is the day, she is ready to take the next bus out of town. I just can't imagine what my life was like before Airedales, easily one of the best things to come into my life.

Cecil Patrick Jr.

Kuta was the neighbor Stephan's dog. He had been purchased to breed with a bull terrier for "pig dog" or pig-hunting dog. That's the most esteemed mix for Hawaiian pig hunters. And dogs in that world are commodities for the most part. Added to this the fact that Stephen was a tragic, but powerful, abusive personality, and you have a creature destined for a dreadful life.

Kuta spent his first year of life tied up to a stake. I could see him only every now and then and there was nothing I could do. Then the door of opportunity opened a crack. The neighbor came over with the dog onto my property where he was grazing his cow. I saw Kuta who was a matted blob, soaking with body fluids but nonetheless, had a gently wagging tail. I was more or less guided not to confront Stephan about Kuta. When he came back a few days later he said, "Look at the dog, it makes me sad." I said, "Oh yes, what's he have?" He said, "Don't know." The next time he came over, I said, "Can I give him a bath?" He grudgingly relented to this relinquishing of control over the situation. I took the boy to my house, gave him the bath, which was a literally nauseating ordeal, but I was happy to be helping him.

After the bath, I took the boy back and the neighbor did not answer the door. At the heart of the matter was that he had lost face.

Kuta was to be in my hands from then on. When Kuta came into my life, he was suffering from a devastating case of "demodectic mange," a condition of thousands of microscopic spiders living in the hair follicles. The disease is accompanied by secondary infection-in Kuta's case, it was Staff. Maggots were cleaning up the dead tissue. He had ten "volcanoes of puss and blood" on his head and neck. One was evident over his brow. His eyes were swollen almost shut and filled with mucus. He had every intestinal worm in the book. His skin had become black and thick like elephant hide. This is a condition called "sebaria" which occurs after intense trauma to the skin. When he arrived, his feces was white. He was so disabled that he couldn't climb stairs or jump in the car for a month and a half after I had started the treatments.

I visualized the dog clean and beautiful and started giving him an Airedale clip right away. Kuta was to go to the vet for the dips, acupuncture and herbs to boost his immune system and other treatments for over a year before he emerged healthy. The vets accepted some trades of my art for the bill which was to come to over $3500. This is, of course, just a part of this story of renaissance and the creator's healing grace!

While I was in Montana having an art exhibition, my dear Airedale companion, Kuta, died unexpectedly at home on Kauai where my friends Billy and Dania were house-sitting. Shortly after I returned, a woman whom I had never met, named Regina, phoned me to say that she had had a very special time with Kuta one day at my home while I was away. She came over and dictated while I jotted down this account. This event had happened a week before he was to "travel on."

"One day I was in a very dark hour in my soul and in a great deal of emotional and physical pain. I was sitting on a chair in the living room. Billy was just about to give me a healing session. Kuta was sitting next to me, and started inching closer and closer. Suddenly I just broke down, completely fell apart, felt all the pain in the world and all the injustice that was threatening to destroy me in that moment. Kuta came still closer-like he couldn't contain himself. He really picked up on my pain, as if he completely felt-not only felt- but was trying with great compassion to comfort me. He absolutely knew what was going on inside of me and I had the feeling that most likely, he had experienced the same total loneliness and pain. Kuta tried to climb on top of me. If he could speak he would have said, "I know exactly how you feel and really want to help you." He was just full of love and caring. He made noises as if he were trying to talk-not whining, but making these talking noises- not like a dog, I mean some dogs are somehow limited in their expression, but Kuta was literally communicating with me on an incredibly deep level of knowingness and had the unmistakably clear intent of really wanting to help.

"Billy was not able to continue with the healing session because of Kuta's intense activity and asked Dania to put him in the bedroom. Then, out of the blue, Billy said that some dogs intentionally pick up and take over all your karma. I felt that Kuta was trying to do just that. After the session Kuta came right back out and joined me again. I know now the history of his own early abandonment and pain and can understand our interaction with even more clarity." September, 1998

A Hui Ho, my precious friend; until we make our circle again. You entered my life with pain and need and a wagging tail and gave to me the chance to give with all my heart, which is the greatest blessing....

Susan Olsen

Today I "sprung" our totally charming ADT out of the pound and dubbed him "Willie." This boy has a magnetic personality. People can't seem to resist him. Let me digress. While still at the pound, I struggled awkwardly to get him in the seat harness for the ride to the kennel-he was totally patient although I know he was thrilled to be out of that concrete and iron cage. This harness has an attachment that doubles as a lead, so after getting him secured, I took him for a walk around the grounds for a sniff-fest. Finally it was time to get in the car and get going and he could barely contain his glee looking forward to the ride. He piled in and cooperated with my hooking things up and off we went. He positioned himself strategically to pick up maximum aire-conditioning and rode through stop and go traffic beautifully. I kept reaching back and scratching head and ears, playing with his feet (no problem), and calling him Willie. He loved the attention.

Thursday my husband or I will meet Laura Post halfway between Austin and Houston and Laura will return to Houston with him where he will receive all of his medical assessment, neutering, and she will foster him. Laura will have much more opportunity to learn about this boy, if he is housetrained, how he is with children, etc. He is a sweet and very handsome Airedale. I noticed that he may have one ear that "marches to a different drummer" but grooming may improve that.

Cheryl Silver

When Jake's previous owner brought him to our house, he stayed for a couple of hours. The big sticking point was going to be Jake's reaction to the cat, Fiona. Now, we've been renovating our old school house for many years, and one of our innovations is the cat door, a tiny door beside the big French door to our front hall. This allows the cat access to the basement (and litter box) without allowing all the heat to escape from the main part of the house to our as yet unrenovated front hallway. On the top of the door frame, in the living room, there is one of those cut-out silhouettes of a cat climbing down, painted black. Fiona decided to make a break for it away from Jake, and ran though the cat door. Jake watched her go, and then noticed the cat on top of the door! He started barking excitedly at it, much to our amusement! My mother-in-law has a similar cut-out cat in her kitchen, and Jake barks at it as well.

He recently noticed the Hamster on one of her rare appearances in our waking hours, driving Jake into a frenzy. He kept running to us, whacking us with his head as if to say "Hey! There's a rodent in that cage!" and running back to her. He was priceless! You know, it just gets better all the time with Jake. He's really a wonderful guy. He's got so much personality. And he and Brandy, who was our only dog for over 12 years, have adapted to each other so well. During the day they sleep together on their two beds put together (this saves all the hassle of them stealing the other's beds). I love to watch them together on our walks, their keen interest in minute inspections of sections of ploughed fields, blades of grass, etc., noses together, shoulder to shoulder. He even likes having her lick peanut butter off his face after he's cleaned out the almost empty container.

I really have to be grateful that Jake's previous owner made the wise decision, after a change of his life circumstance, to give Jake up to a more suitable home. The poor chap was almost in tears when he left Jake here; it was a real sacrifice for him to give up this wonderful pal.

Stephanie Coulshaw

(Before being sent to a home, a rescue is evaluated for temperament, training, and personality.)

I just spent the morning with Chug, whose new name according to the folks at Irwin Animal Hospital in Albion, Michigan, is Sampson. Personally, he will always be Chug to me! I hung up my Orvis field jacket in the Xray room of the clinic and went and got Chug. He is big and strong for a dog full of heartworms! But not at all aggressive to humans, unless you count his promptly going over and taking a leak on the aforementioned Orvis field jacket! Yep, that's how he introduced himself to me! My fault though, he is not neutered and that jacket has been on the rounds with Bilbo and Frodo.

After spending a few minutes in the closed quarters of the Xray room, we proceeded out to a nearby field on a long training lead for some clicker training. Chug is very smart. He quickly associated the click with the delivery of either the freeze dried liver or chicken in my training pouch and was sitting about 80% of the time without physical assist in a matter of minutes (the other 20% of the time he was jumping up in my face to deliver kisses). Despite the heart worm he lead me to all corners of the field, excitedly sniffing all smells and repeating the process initially done to my jacket on every interesting spot he found. The field was fenced by post and rail and he even scrunched under it to follow up on a smell outside the fence and came back to a lure (chicken) when called.

After about an hour of clicker training, it seemed like he might be getting tired (I know I was!), so we returned to the Xray room for the acid tests. I got out a long rope toy of Bilbo's to play tug of war, but Chug didn't really know what to do with it, a sad tribute to his early life. I then got out an 8 inch rawhide which he quickly latched on to with his big jaws and we proceeded to play tug of war with no growling at all and he let me take it away from him several times. His human bite inhibition is fine; several times when I gave him freeze dried treats, he would "puppy nip" at my fingers and stop. Believe me, I have seen worse, much worse dogs who responded to clickers and compassion. He permitted me to handle him all over with no hint of aggression. He loves ear and under-neck scratches in particular. The closest thing to aggression was his snorting in reply to the snort of the pot bellied pig we passed on the way in and out of the kennel (I actually think it was more of a "hello"). He is to be treated for the heart worm, and any other parasites, then have the eye entropion surgery, and then will be placed in a loving home!

Skip Barcy

Back in April of '98 I rescued a 6 month old female Airedale named Sophie from Joey Finneran of the Delaware Valley Airedale Rescue. Sophie had some rough beginnings. In her first home she was getting into trouble on a regular basis and proved to be difficult to control. Her welcome ran dry when she broke free from her crate one day and ravaged the house. During her romp of freedom, she attacked an answering machine and ingested the cassette tape inside.

This was the end of the line for poor Sophie. Her owners took her to the vet where she had surgery to remove the remnants of the tape.

Joey Finneran of Del Valley Rescue picked Sophie up from the hospital and began the foster process. That's where Jocelyn my wife, Bailey my 3 year old Wheaten Terrier, and I came in. We had been searching for a rescue Wheaten for a long time, almost 2 years. I had finally given up on rescuing a Wheaten since the rescue folks never seemed to have a dog that fit our lifestyle. So I turned to Airedale Rescue and two weeks later there was a Del Val Rescue Rep at my house checking out the situation. They found my family as a suitable recipient for an ADT and a week later I had a rambunctious pup bounding around my yard.

Things were a little rough at the start. Sophie suffered a few bouts with urinary tract infections and had some chronic diarrhea, but I found her to be a good dog. Sophie is now 13 months old, she loves her older brother Bailey the Wheaten, and she is a well adjusted young lady. She doesn't destroy the house; she hasn't eaten any electronic devices and seems to be well past all the medical issues. She is a little goofy at times, which, until I subscribed to AIREDALE-L thought was a bit strange. Now I see that she is a perfectly normal ADT.

All the warnings that she came with seemed to go away on their own. She has fit in great with the family. She did take ownership of my EZ Chair. So now when it's time to settle in and watch some football, the Wheaten lies on the couch, the Airedale curls up in the EZ Chair, and -you may have guessed it-I am on the floor. All in all she was a great find. Now I have two running partners and two fishing partners whom I can always count on to be at my side no matter what. ADTs really are marvelous animals, and they deserve a second chance with an owner who understands what they are all about.

Mike Marzo

One evening Phoebe was tossed from the window of a moving car on a Miami, FL city street. She hit the pavement, and tried to get up and run after the car from which she had been thrown, but was hurt and unable to go far. She was taken in by a couple in Miami who wanted to keep her, but Phoebe proved to be a real Alpha female and started creating problems with the other canines in the family. They released her to Airedale Rescue. Phoebe moved in with us and has been learning to get along with our pack of Airedales.

At our club's Christmas party I was approached by a new club member who had heard about Phoebe and thought it sounded like the dog that had been stolen from her Miami backyard the year before. When she showed me photographs of her lost Airedale, there was no doubt it was the same dog! This lady had recently purchased a new Airedale puppy, and because she was unable to have more than one dog, she decided to leave Phoebe with Airedale rescue.

I will be placing her in a new home soon. I would not place her over the Christmas holidays-that is not a good time for a dog to go into a new home. There is generally too much confusion in the household at that time to devote the time required to let a new dog settle in.

Sally Schnellman

Photon arrived at his forever home tonight after two long days of travel with various Lindas (Linda Baake, Linda Taylor, and Linda Klingerman). He was a real trooper throughout the trip, winning everyone's heart with his sweetness and dignity. He is even older than I expected. He moves rather slowly and from behind resembles an old man shuffling around in baggy pajamas and corduroy scuffs. His eyes and attitude are bright, though; he IS an Airedale. The first thing Photon did when he arrived was wander about the house, checking out EACH and EVERY ITEM within his range. He was like an old colonel. Couch-check. Bookcase-check. Plant in corner-check. Not for peeing upon. Check. Hardwood floor. No problem. Treats in female Upright's coat pocket. Jolly good. Couch with dog aroma. Must be the Canine Cabana. Check. Corners-check. Nothing lurking here. Or here. Check. Water bowl-check!

After he'd satisfied himself that all was in order, he condescended to wag his tail at John and get some Quality Attention. John, after living with one woman and two bitches (or is that three bitches) was amazed to discover that this dog does have a penis. He also said we need to learn about the special needs of Old Dogs now (Check). Photon also inspected the yard. He had no trouble with the steps down to the big yard and anointed many of our bushes. Rita and Ellie seem to know that he is not as boisterous and strong as they and treat him with the respect and gentleness he is due. This, I believe, is Rita's doing. She KNOWS, and Ellie is following her lead. (Rita did, however, drool all over him as they were getting acquainted at Linda Klingermans!) When he wandered to the front yard, Photon encountered Fluffy One. (We have two white spitz-type dogs next door whose names we can never keep straight, so John calls them Fluffy One and Fluffy Two. Fluffy One comes over regularly to play with Rita in the back yard.) ANYWAY, when Photon saw Fluffy One, he drew himself up tall and dignified, and minced over to The Fluff, as if to say "This, sir, is MY YARD. You must ask permission to enter." They sniffed, Fluffy sort of backed down. Photon said "Permission to enter granted, Sir Fluff."

He has stationed himself for the time being in the Grande Hallway, which puts him at the epicenter of all the activity in the house right now. (It's about 4' by 6' and connects the LR, kitchen, Puter room, bedroom, bath and stairway.) John is infatuated with this dignified old guy (and so am I). This is a good match! Another Spare Dale finds a forever home. He will be pampered and respected for the rest of his days.

Gena Welch

Last night, Photon was seized by a fierce PLAYSPASM and when that happens, what a puppy he can be! The girls were outside and I took a little time to give the Colonel my undivided attention, petting him, massaging him, and telling how wonderful he is. Suddenly, he got up, pranced into the living room and began running around. He even accomplished a couple of geriatric play bows. We played "Toss the Little Blue Man" and "Catch the Rolling Kong," and "Lob that Huge Bone and Watch Mom Worry About the TV set" and for a while, we simply danced a Happydance, facing one another and smiling. He seemed to be in complete glee, but soon got a bit tired and settled down. I would not trade these special moments with my very experienced Senior Rescue for a million puppies. Please, please, if seeking a SpareDale, give these old ones a look.

Gena Welch

All of the dogs I have fostered so far have been strays. Gypsy has been with me for the last month while she recovered, first from her spay surgery, and then from the removal of three mammary tumors. Some of you know what bad shape she was in when I got her. At first we thought she might be about 5, then we guessed 8, now we think probably about 10 and probably a puppy mill mamma, churning out two litters a year. She could barely walk because her hips were so weak and her nails so long. It was touch and go for a while whether I might have to euthanize her. However, there was a certain sparkle in her eye and I just couldn't do it. Wonderful Rescue said to have the tumors removed and analyzed. Great news-they were benign and fully contained and we have been taking her on numerous walks each day and giving her a combo of buffered aspirin, glucosamine and glycoflex. The last two days she has started out the morning by doing playbows and pawslaps and Grrrs and Barks with my two youngsters-all tails wagging-a great maelstrom of black and tan in the middle of my living room. She has actually trotted around the entire yard on our pre-breakfast walk.

When I send her medical information to her new home, I will also send a list of the quirks I have observed while she has been here. One of them is that she walks around the house staring up, which might cause some concern to her new owner if not explained. This started after she looked up one day and discovered Curtis, my Amazon parrot. She is obsessed by Curtis and now looks up at the entire house, wondering what fascinating creature she might discover next.

Sidney Hardie

Maggie is our beloved "survivor." We have patiently been working with her to help her come back into being a pet. The good Lord only knows what she had to endure prior to the Rescue Angels entering her life but we knew with lots of love and encouragement she'd come around. Well she's now doing those Airedale things. Her first love is Brian. She fell in love with him at first sight, although I am a close second. Just as my Cody chose me to be guided by him gently clamping down on my arm, Maggie is now doing this routinely to Brian. "Dad, Dad, come see this. Dad, Dad come get me another cookie." It brought tears to my eyes the first time I witnessed this act. I had to explain to Brian what it all meant. I also told him not every person gets this, only the chosen one.

This morning we are spring cleaning which means running the vac all that many more places and scrubbing and buffing floors. Well, Maggie has been keeping a very close eye on the power head (central vac). The butt up, legs down hop, hop back and a quick bark at it. No attacks-yet. Now she is just getting up on whatever piece of furniture doesn't have something stacked on it (books, other chairs, her dog basket, her toy box, the like...)-watching, watching and cocking that CUTEST head back and forth. This morning when we were snuggling she just couldn't stand it. Yup. Right up on the bed she leaped and of course had to get that big ole head right down between us and then PLOP so she was in the middle, her head on the pillows and just laughing and giggling as we were. I see now every day there is a little more of ADT coming out. It is delightful. Now if she can just keep from (re)discovering counter surfing, we'll be just perfect!

Judie Burcham

About 31/2 months ago, I got my foster 'dale, Gracie. She had been found wandering the streets and was taken to a shelter in the next county. She had a very nasty wound on her side, foxtails in her feet, severely infected ears, kennel cough, low spirits, glazed over eyes, and a terrible limp. She was also overweight. She is about 1 inch taller than Bacchus who weighs 45 LB, and she weighs 75 lbs. Just last week, the vet detected a very slight heart murmur.

Now her feet have healed and the limp is gone. Her ears, though they will require lifelong treatment, no longer seem to bother her. I think they are permanently scarred and thickened. The vet determined that she had a very low thyroid level and so, with medication, she's regained energy. Her eyes have cleared. She is still overweight. The wound on her side, however, has not healed. She has been on antibiotics the entire time I've had her and the infection is somewhat better but still flares up and periodically oozes lots of pus and blood (ick!). They've probed for foxtails and found none. The vets were reluctant to re-open the wound, an infected surgical incision, but I suspect they will do that soon, since it's flaring up again. But because it's much more localized now, it won't be as big a deal.

Watching the changes in Gracie has been the most amazing thing. Her eyes went from a strange glassy stare (hard to describe) to the typical Airedale eyes we all know and love. Her ears used to hang down and now one looks perfectly set and the other-well, it still hangs a bit. From behind, she used to look a bit like an elephant with a lot of loose folds hanging in the crotch. And she trotted around like a woman with her control-top pantyhose only halfway pulled-up, the crotch hanging at the knees and the control-top squeezing the thighs together, making running very difficult. But now she's tightened up and pulled up her pantyhose. And her spirits? She's all a-wag, all the time. Well, almost. She still doesn't enjoy having Bacchus biting her hindquarters (I suspect she's a bit arthritic, too) but she holds her own. When I've been away, even if only for a few minutes, I'm welcomed home in the most heartwarming way -she spins and jumps, though only a few inches, and her whole body wags. She is sweet, gentle, and good. She rarely leaves my side-and I want to keep her!

Kim Kamrath.

Miles is an orphan from Cleveland, OH. His life owner, Barbara, died of breast cancer last fall. She had asked that all her animals be euthanized upon her death. Her daughter didn't follow her wishes. Her daughter saved and placed three dogs, four cats, and several birds that Miles grew up with in the small suburban home. They couldn't place Miles. His groomer, Jerry, who had cared for him since he was 91/2 weeks old, told me that he and Barbara were the only two people that Miles would let in the house if nobody was home. Miles can have an attitude. He was obviously the master of the house.

I think that Miles had trial placements at some homes. Last October, he was returned to his vet. clinic. I think they were supposed to have put him down but they couldn't do it. He is a sweet 'dale once he drops his attitude with you. They tried ads and placements. He became the kennel dog with free run in the upstairs kennel area.

In February, they contacted an Ohio 'dale hunt club. He was too old for them. One of their members got a hold of Sandi with ATRA. Sandi had her moments with Miles. Miles and Dan mixing it up, Jake and Miles mixing it up. All 4 of them getting into it. Jake backing Miles into the bathroom. He raided the kitchen at Sandi's and he and Jake had a food orgy that still marks Sandi's kitchen carpet! Don't get me wrong. They had lots and lots of fun. Miles can be a blast when he wants to be! He doesn't run out of open doors. He rides in cars very well and waits to be let out. He walks quite well on lead, especially with a choke collar. He sits at curbs and waits to be told OK to cross. BUT he can get in stubborn cross bitey moods when being protective or over food. I have scars to prove it.

You see, Miles opens refrigerator doors. Sandi's, ours at home, and the cottage up north. The one at the house, that he is alone with most, is now held closed with a strong bungee cord. Velcro didn't do the job! His first morning alone he broke into the fridge and ate 3/4 of a large deep dish pizza, a Chinese dinner, 2 lbs of ham/turkey/ cheeses, bread, and 1 LB of butter. He went back for seconds in the afternoon! He is not fat. He has a thing about food. He is first in line all the time!

Kirk Nims

Fergie is a 7-year-old TINY Airedale spayed female with what can only be described as a domineering personality. She had to leave her first home because she bit a two-year-old child. The owners were kind enough to realize that the bite came from their own inability to properly civilize Ferg and got in touch with Airedale Rescue, which is where I came in. I fostered Fergie for about 4 months while working on some of her behavior problems, getting her weight down where it belonged (she came to me weighing 48 pounds and left at 42-looking very svelte with a new haircut), and trying to find just the right placement for her. I moaned and groaned on the list a few times about problems I was having with her, but I also almost fell in love with her because she could be very endearing (and SMART-I could have made a competitive obedience dog out of her if I had gotten her at a younger age and kept her).

Fergie is living with a wonderful young couple in Akron, Ohio (no kids and none planned). She went from being the smallest dog in my 3-dog household to being the biggest dog in their 3-dog household. They have an older Havanese neutered male and a fairly young unneutered Tibetan terrier male who is a show dog. I just called them last week to see how things are going and they are absolutely delighted with Fergie. They are dog-savvy enough that they know how to keep her from totally ruling the roost and she is apparently a total angel compared to their Tibetan terrier, who seems to have a genuine temperament problem and has bitten Amy a couple of times. They have a fenced yard, take all 3 dogs for long walks, and Jeff comes home for lunch, so the pups gets lots of attention.

According to Amy, Ferg has gotten very attached to Jeff, who knows how to play with an Airedale. Fergie had a flare-up of her recurring bladder infection right after she got there (I think stress can bring this on), but that cleared up on antibiotics and she now gets a cranberry capsule every day. It's a great placement and I'm very pleased.

Barbara Mann

I called Fergie's adoptive parents (Jeff and Amy) Thursday to see how things have been going. I am ecstatic about these folks-they couldn't be a better match for her. So far, here's a list of events:

1. Fergie got another bladder infection and peed all over their bed (their BED? Clearly she has moved in!). Their reaction was to worry dreadfully about her, take her to their very good vet, get her on antibiotics which get mixed with canned dog food (I used to just stuff pills down her throat!), and go to the Internet to read up on bladder infections.

2. Fergie had a gorgeous haircut just before they got her. They live in Akron, OH, which is a little colder and with more snow than here. They were afraid she'd get too cold on their walks, so they bought her a jacket to wear.

3. In a play session with Jeff, Fergie bit him. But he says it was an accident. (I think I probably know better. She's a brat and she wasn't getting her way.)

4. She's started humping Wally, their Tibetan terrier, who is an intact. Jeff and Amy both understand that this is dominance behavior. Wally is perplexed.

They adore her! I expect she'll have them serving her caviar on a silver platter before summer. I am going to tell them about the list and let them know how to join. I may get them a copy of Houses Full of Laughter.

Barbara Mann

Piper's Story

R*escue volunteers normally do their work quietly, picking up Airedales in answer to a phone call, checking them out of shelters, rushing them to the vet when necessary without panicking. Once in a while an announcement appears* *on the list about a special 'dale needing a home. Meanwhile, list members help with donations and offers of transport and fostering, as needed. The appeal to help "spring" Piper, who was due to be euthanized, was not only answered with instant action by hundreds of list members all over the world; but the news media also proved to be a powerful tool in saving her life. Here is Piper's story as it appeared on Airedale-L, except that the names of the community college and its officials are now designated by initials.*

There is a dire situation at KW Community College. An Airedale needs help! A young female ADT named Piper has been used in the lab for Vet Tech training. Mary Gade, Airedale Rescue in IA, has been attempting to rescue Piper for some months now. She has gotten the run-around and several stalls. Now the latest news is that the college has deemed Piper "unadoptable." They are going to euthanize her.

Several people in authority at KW have refused to allow Airedale Rescue to help Piper. Mary and I have written letters to N, president of the college. We have pleaded for him to allow Rescue to take Piper and have her evaluated by Airedale-experienced people. So far, we have gotten nowhere! Airedale Rescue is waiting to take custody of Piper. We have the financial and professional resources to do whatever it takes to give this young Airedale a new start in life. Mary is exploring the use of the local media to help save Piper. She has also contacted an attorney or two, plus several animal rights groups.

We may lose this battle for Piper's life but we will go down fighting! Will you Listers help? I'm not exactly sure WHAT more to do but the email address for President N is: (listed). And maybe a cc to The Cedar Rapids Gazette (address listed). Be my guest; write them. Plead for Piper to be given a chance to live with people who understand what an Airedale is all about.

Perhaps N should be encouraged to issue a "stay of execution" until he can investigate this matter fully. Piper has resided in this lab for a year now. Certainly a few days to check on details and verify our credentials could not hurt! We are open to any and all suggestions on how to save Piper. We appreciate your support!

Carol Domeracki, Airedale Terrier Rescue and Adoption, Treasurer
ATCA Rescue Committee Midwest Coordinator

(Note: Listmembers immediately flooded the President's office with calls and e-mails urging him forcefully yet courteously to release Piper and telling him more than he ever wanted to know about the Airedale temperament, Airedale Rescue, ethics, responsibility, and the repercussions of not releasing her.)

Piper was donated to KW at the age of 5 months. She was purchased from a puppymill in Illinois by an elderly woman who was told by an obedience trainer that Piper was impossible. She was advised to get rid of Piper, hence the donation to KW's veterinary technician training program at the age of 5 months.

When I found out there was an Airedale at KW, I called for confirmation and was told that she would be ready for adoption in September. I went to visit her, and found a very quiet, depressed, forlorn little girl. I was also told she was not doing well in the program. I told them I had an approved home and wanted to adopt her, and explained Airedale Rescue. They were to get in touch with me. I called again and was told she was not going to be available, due to an intestinal problem, possibly Giardia. They were treating it and she would have to stay until the first week in December. I told them I would be happy to take her myself and give her the medication. They would not send her out of the college while she was on medication.

In December I was told she would have to stay for the next session, and she could not be adopted until the end of February. When I called last Tuesday to see if I could get her, I was told she was not adoptable and was going to be put down. I ask WHY and was told she had behavioral problems and bad hips. I asked if she had dysplasia [a common problem among large-breed, poorly bred dogs] and was told she did not. I asked if her intestinal problem was due to

Giardia, and was told she had never had Giardia. I asked if her behavioral problems were aggression and told no, and that the vet techs were upset that she was going to be put down.

I almost begged them to let me adopt her, telling them I would sign anything they needed relinquishing them of any responsibility. I was told she came from a puppymill and was not mentally stable. I gave up and came home. I couldn't sleep that night, and decided to find out who determined her fate. I went over the department heads and called the Dean of Agriculture. He called back and stated that he had conferred with the staff, and that they would not "adopt that dog out." It was something that they did not feel comfortable with. (That is on the answering machine and almost an exact quote).

The rest is history. I called Carol, and she said to go for it and told me Airedale Rescue would back me all the way. We had nothing to lose at that point. My biggest fear was that they would put her down out of spite. Carol posted to you guys; I called a reporter at the Gazette and an acquaintance who is an attorney and animal rights activist. She called the animal rights people, I called all of my contacts asking them to call the president and we were on a roll! I must tell you I forewarned the Dean that he might want to reconsider his decision and that they were going to tangle with a force unknown to him. (He thought he was dealing with a gray-haired, sick old lady. Boy did he get a surprise!) That was yesterday and we truly didn't think we would find her alive.

Last night I got a one line email from President N, advising me I would hear from the vice president or the dean in the morning. I thought maybe we had struck a nerve. Late this morning I received a call from the dean, and honey was dripping from his lips. He wondered how I was feeling and I told him I was sick. He said he had some good news for me and that I could pick up Piper today. He also asked if I would call off the media. I told him I would do what I could but that it was already in motion, and reminded him that he had been forewarned. KW agreed to release her after she had been checked by a veterinarian and we had signed release papers.

Mary Gade

PIPER IS HOME WITH ME. We are both exhausted! KW and the Gazette have issued a plea to STOP the emails. Their computers are about to CRASH. I CAN'T BEGIN TO TELL YOU HOW WONDERFUL YOU ARE, AND HOW WONDERFUL PIPER IS. WE DID IT. I am almost in a state of shock. It never would have happened without all of you! The letters did it! You saved a wonderful little female, whose life will begin NOW. They were adamant that we couldn't have this Airedale yesterday morning! They didn't have a clue whom they were dealing with. You are a mighty bunch.

They released her to our vet about 3:00 PM with my attorney in attendance They wanted her out of there as fast as we could get her. The Gazette followed us to get the story and was waiting at the vet's office. Their story will be in the paper tomorrow and we are on the TV news as I write. Piper is a delight and a little ham. She even gave the reporters and cameraman kisses. She is one of happiest little girls I have ever seen.

She got a clean bill of health from the vet who saw NO behavioral problems! Remember we were told she was not adoptable, and not healthy yesterday? That was a total, complete crock. Forgive me for rambling but it has been a very emotional two days.

The stop at the vets was a real bummer. They had to draw blood and we had trouble holding her down. Certainly not a normal reaction. She has had more than her share of that procedure. KW College wished they had never heard of Airedale Rescue! What a mighty bunch you guys are. I just wish all of you could see how wonderful she is. And how HAPPY! I love the whole world right now.

Mary Gade, Airedale Rescue, Cedar Rapids, Iowa

I am sitting here basking in the wonderful letters from all of you! Piper, Clancy, and Dolly [Mary's ADTs] finally settled in. I appreciate all of the wonderful things you are saying about me, but I have done nothing more than any of you would have done in the same circumstances. Actually, all of you guys did more than I. There is no way Piper would be sleeping here beside me tonight without you. I am an old gray-haired sickly lady, living on a hill. Not much of a threat to anyone, wouldn't you say! Well, with all of you with me, we moved a mountain, like Pip Smith said. I am so proud to be part of you.

The people in the animal rights groups can't believe what has happened. Most of them don't have a fraction of the support and help I have had. And Carol! What a piece of work SHE is! I had all the support and encouragement I could have asked for. There are not many around like her! What a lady. I wish you could all know her as I do.

I was greatly helped by Laurie Stone, all breed rescue person, animal rights activist and now friend. She contacted many animal rights groups, friends with clout, and the news media. She also prepared the release papers, acting as our attorney while dealing with KW. She accompanied us when we picked up Piper, and was with us when we took her to the vet. And our own lister Gale Ford, DVM, helped our cause, more than I can say. She called from Montana and she pulled a bunch of strings. Many thanks to Gale, too. I will never forget all of you, nor the last two days. Piper is stretched out sleeping like an angel, and so will I be doing soon.

Mary Gade

WOW! Piper is alive and starting her new life! Simply unbelievable! Normally I'm an optimist but I considered this a lost cause. Was I wrong! Thank doG! I know that many of you were with me as I read Mary's triumphant post, tears in my eyes. That Mary Gade! A truly wonderful, strong-willed lady. She wouldn't give up! And neither would you! A huge "Thank-You" to each and everyone of you who sent email on Piper's behalf. Words simply can't express the joy that is felt tonight all over the world. I am not a member of the List but I certainly support you all in your Airedale efforts. You are a formidable force. (I just have to remember to stay on your good side!)

Oh, and please stop emailing KW Community College. They got the point!

Carol Domeracki,
ATRA Treasurer, ATCA Rescue Committee
Midwest Coordinator

Piper couldn't be sweeter disposition-wise, but she tries to protect herself by taking a hold of hands and arms with her mouth. The more you try to correct her, the harder she fights and bites down. Not a BITE bite, but I can see it would scare the h*ll out of someone that wasn't savvy. She is suspicious of what is going to be done to her. Can you blame her? She is learning after less than a week, that self-defense is not necessary and I am not going to hurt her. If you substitute something else in her mouth and praise her, she immediately stops and gives you kisses! She needs to go to someone special who understands her and what she has been through. In my opinion, she has learned this behavior out of self defense and it is going to take a while to change. If you get tough with her, she just tries harder, so that route is not going to work. You can't shame her either. (She has NO shame.) She looks at you with a mischievous kind of gleam in those beautiful brown eyes and I hardly keep a straight face. [Ed. note: the aforementioned behaviors are typical of most ADTs.] It is so funny, as if she is saying, "OK, NOW what are you gonna try to do!" You can just see the mischief coming out of those eyes.

It is a miracle that she is not mean, and the little darlin' doesn't have a mean bone in her body. The more love and praise we give her, the sweeter she is. She was in my lap this morning, ALL 60 SOME POUNDS, and settled in but had to reached up to kiss my ear every once in a while. She adores my husband Milt. I think she likes men better than women. Dolly and Clancy were in their crates and it was peaceful. At times like this I think about keeping her, but do try to be realistic because of my d*mn health.

I hate to tell you this, but I think she will do better in a home without other dogs or with someone who realizes she is still just a puppy! She loves dogs but she is the wild child when around them. She wants to mount them and of course chew and it seems to bring out the worst in everyone! I am sure this will change in time. She is changing every day. I thank God we saved her.

Mary Gade
(Piper moved from Mary's home to that of Skip and Becky Barcy for further fostering and training.)

Well last night was a biggy here; I gave up my recliner and the OSU/Det Titans NCAA game to introduce Piper to her new family. Annette contacted me and indicated a transplanted English family, with older elementary and secondary age kids, and an ADT named Angus (4yo male neut.) were interested in Piper. The family wondered if they could come and meet Piper last night. To make a long story short, all got along famously and they hope to pick up Piper next weekend after they move into their new home. Piper's new mom was absolutely aghast that such a sweet dog could have been the object of training in a vet tech school. As I write this, there are 3 contented Airedales working desperately to get their tongues into the Kongs and the treats out! Earlier they each got a cow ear as a special treat. Bilbo and Frodo immediately sat down and began wolfing the treat down, but not Piper-she had to toss hers in the air a couple of times and play bow to it before finally deciding it was OK to eat.

Skip and Becky Barcy

[The following was received from Annette of ATRA who delivered Piper to her new family.] Skip, I couldn't have hoped for a better match for Piper than Angus (6 yr. old neutered male Airedale), Nadia (9 yr. old girl), Louis (16 yr. old boy), Linda and Steve (adults). This wonderful family just moved into their new home yesterday yet wanted to take Piper in right away so Angus wouldn't have the upper hand. Ha! Angus is very sweet-natured and not at all aggressive over anything.

Nadia was my only worry but she took control of Piper right off the bat. It was Nadia who kept hold of Piper's leash inside and kept her from jumping up on all the rest of us. We witnessed Piper trying to gnaw the corner of a wood table, Nadia corrected her; Piper trying to steal Angus's food, Nadia corrected her, on and on. Nadia seems to have the right tone (not shrill like most kids) and is quick so the dog knows what's O.K. and what's not.

The back yard is lovely and Louis gets home from school by 2:30 p.m. so Piper will only be crated from around 9 a.m. to then. Linda gets home at 3:30 with Nadia following. I think this will work out fine. Dear Angus is well-trained and the family will lose the crate just as soon as possible. Linda refused to use one when Angus was a pup. Skip sent Piper with an assortment of goodies and her own brand of dog food. The family have our book Second Hand Dog to refer to, all of our numbers, and I'm just 10 minutes away!

Annette

Piper is really a very good dog in their opinion. Linda has said that since she is a female, you must deal with her differently from a male dog. Approach her gently and use distractions, not yelling or harsh measures to stop her from doing naughty things. I wish you could hear her explain her theories with that lovely British accent!

Piper has been digging enormous holes in the garden (they mean back yard!) so Steve has been burying crushed red chili peppers to keep her from digging again in the same place. Piper still takes everything outdoors and buries it immediately. Linda digs up the fresh holes, takes the toy or chew treat back inside and washes and dries it for another day. It was too crowded in the master bed for 2 humans and 2 ADT's so now they pet-gate both Angus and Piper in the family room at night for sleeping. They abandoned the crate (it's in their garage) weeks ago and Piper is on the honor system in the house when they are home and pet-gated in the family room with Angus when they go to work/school. Linda was under tremendous stress trying to finish her thesis and now it's being typed. She sounds exhausted but even so not at all stressed out over Piper. Angus and Piper have been bonded like two peas right from the start. Linda said Piper really wears the poor old boy out! They are eating together and Piper has had no tummy trouble or diarrhea. The kids say she's wonderful.

Linda and Steve are already worrying about their vacation in August. They want the two dogs boarded together in a kennel but worry that Piper might feel she's being abandoned so they may try and get family to stay in the house with both dogs. They keep repeating that Piper is a very lovely girl and they love her! I wish we had more applicants like these!

Christie Williams

CHAPTER TEN
JP's Chapter

THE DEATH OF John P. Van Cleave in the spring of 1999 after nearly a year's battle with melanoma was the first human loss in our list family. An attorney living in Lookout Mountain, Georgia, JP had a true Airedale outlook: wicked, forgiving, and full of love. This is John's chapter because we miss him and we know there will be no more posts from him. His lasting tribute will be the laughter these stories provoke.

Anybody ever been to a Dog Blessing? Or, "Blessing of the Pets" as it was called here. Well, let me tell you. Not long ago the teenagers came home from their youth group at the church excited about the dog blessing they were going to have as a fund-raiser. My first reaction was, "Here we go again, with the Church with its hand deeply into my pocket." But I warmed to the idea. After all, it certainly couldn't hurt, and if it worked, think of the money that would be saved in obedience training alone!

Soon enough, I was getting excited myself. Murphy, our Airedale, is a pretty good dog, but to be totally honest, he does have a few bad habits that a blessing might take care of. Now the dachshund, he's an altogether different story. Doc, AKA Little Hitler, is really more in need of an exorcism; but a blessing might be a good start.

So the big day finally comes. Sunday afternoon we all pile into the car to get these dogs some religion. A big crowd is waiting, no doubt hoping for similar results. Seemed like the annual rabies clinic, lots of barking dogs but, strangely, no fights. The dogs must have known where they were. This was great. I was certain that once

Murphy had a clear understanding of Doggie Heaven-and that in all likelihood it would be me who would have to punch his ticket to get there-well it would just be smooth sailing from here on in. Right? So finally it was time to start the service. Murphy plopped himself down in the churchyard and started to lick himself. Doc (neutered 8 years ago) mounted him (The vet says it's a power thing and has nothing to do with sex-sort of like rape-great, really great). Come on guys, this is CHURCH! Oh well, this is why we are here.

So the assistant gets out his guitar and we sing about all creatures great and small, and then we pray, then the priest talks about what a cool guy St. Augustine was, patron saint of animals and all, and come on, the BLESSING, remember? Whoops, almost forgot. They had to pass the plate, and it's Sunday afternoon, and I have no cash. Run to the car and get a roll of quarters, more than I had intended, but what the heck, it's going to be worth every penny. So finally it's time for the blessing.

Do you know what that priest did? He sort of held up his hand and almost apologetically, practically whispering, says something that I guess was a blessing. I think he was embarrassed about the whole thing, afraid someone might be watching. I'm thinking, what a rip, where do I get my money back, and the priest, robes flowing, is ducking into the church, plate in hand. Now this is NOT what I had in mind! I figured we'd get a little more individual attention. Sort of like the priest would grab Murphy on either side of the head and say "Be BLESSED!" Kind of like Oral Roberts used to do with the BE HEALED routine. With Doc, I figured Father would have to throw him around a little bit. And this is it? That's all? How are these dogs supposed to understand the facts of life with a wimpy blessing like that? I heard later that the "fund raiser" was a great success. Harrruuumph. Later another priest told me that in seminary they teach that you're not supposed to bless animals because, I was told, "They don't have souls." Don't have souls??!! Guess he never met an Airedale.

* * *

Mattie at 9 months is guilty of all the usual Airedale sins, and counter surfing is perhaps her most favorite. She has a trick that would really be annoying if it weren't so unique. In addition to the usual meats, vegetables, and cheeses, she also steals milk-in the glass. Somehow the little monster can pick up the glass with her teeth, carry it out of the kitchen, set it down and drink the milk, out of the glass, without breaking the glass or even knocking it over. Hasn't yet spilled a drop. Granted, the glasses haven't been full, but still. She's done this three times. Impressed?

* * *

We've had a Lab since Easter Sunday when we "rescued" Roscoe from my niece who, of all things, breeds Labs. Seems he was supposed to be a stud (still is, if you ask me) but his tail had too much curl and his muzzle was too long. Maybe. But to my untrained eye, he is a beautiful animal. So we brought the big lug home to see how he'd relate to Mattie and the rest of the neighborhood. True, a Lab is the very antithesis of an Airedale. His personality is, shall we say, limited; he's hardly mischievous, wouldn't think of chewing a shoe; and, yes, he makes a wonderful area rug. He's a chocolate, and goes very well with our color scheme.

I have to say that he does very well in keeping up with Mattie and the other Airedale (another Roscoe) in the neighborhood. In fact, I think the breeds complement each other quite well. The Airedales are expanding his horizons enormously. He's learning to wrestle, even though he always loses, and he's teaching them about chasing tennis balls, even though he always wins. Can't say he's learned everything about being an Airedale, but he's making progress toward becoming an Aire-lab. He'll get into a tug-a war, but he still hasn't learned to verbalize like an Airedale. Still the strong, silent type.

If only he would teach Mattie just a little about being a Lab. Just once I'd like to wake up to her saying "Good morning, Master. What can I do for you today?" Just dreaming. Sorry.

* * *

Advice on peculiarities of owning dogs in the South? What an interesting thought. Until now, it's never occurred to me that there might be something uniquely "southern" about Mattie. She was born almost ten months ago in South Carolina, not really too close to Fort Sumter, but certainly in the same state, and close enough to have an opinion. So just to test the theory, I whistled "Dixie" and her reaction was immediate! She raised her head, looked at me intently, then she cocked her head to one side. Amazing! Instant recognition.

Next, just to confirm the obvious, I got out an old Confederate flag that my Dad had intended to wave when his first male grandchild was born. As she turned out to be a Katie, the flag was still in the wrapper, never unfurled. As Mattie was relaxing in the foyer, I brought out the flag and she snapped to Attention, began barking, and even took hold of a corner, wanting to wave it herself. Unbelievable. Mattie, Daughter of the Old South. This is indeed important, and should probably be reported to some professor at Ole Miss.

OK, the final test. "Tell me, Miss Mattie, was it slavery, or was it industrial/agricultural tensions?" "Frankly, kind sir, I don't give a damn." Holy Cow! Wonder if General Lee had "one of them Aredales?"

John in NW Georgia (not far from Chigger Hill)

* * *

From Debbie (Kiwi) Carley

All of the neighborhood dogs seemed to gather at the VanCleave residence. Some of the dogs knew how to open the gates, he once told me, and it was not uncommon to have a pack of pets outside waiting for Mattie to go out and join in the mischief of the day. His other two dogs were well mannered and calm. And then there was Mattie!

There is one story which he enjoyed a lot. One day last year, one of his neighbors was getting married in an outdoor ceremony. It was a perfect day with a blue sky and light breeze. Everyone in the neighborhood was gathered for this happy occasion. During the ceremony, just at the crucial part of exchanging vows, Miss Mattie and another neighborhood dog decided to crash the wedding ceremony after they had gone for a swim in the lake and rolled in mud! JP said he was just so surprised by her appearance he didn't know what to do. The pastor continued with the vows even after they were all blanketed with a light film of dog mud. He told me this was "classic Mattie" behavior.

* * *

Dadgummit! Doggonnit! Golldurnit!...or maybe just plain old DAMMIT, Mattie!! I've just about HAD it with you. You steal one more stick of butter and I'm gonna cook YOU instead of the turkey. Got it??!! This Airedale is butter-obsessed. I can't butter a piece of toast without her sneaking up behind, and SCHLUCK, she's got the BUTTER (again) and RUN, away with the prize. Actually the RUN is more like a victory trot, sort of heaving as she goes. SCHLUCK, SCHLUCK, gotta get the butter down, wrapper and all, before he tries to retrieve it. What's the use? Ever tried to remove a stick of butter from between two tightly clenched Airedale jaws? Can't be done. Other than that, Happy Thanksgiving to all.

* * *

The call came through at the office. "Mattie's got a rooster!" Michele said breathlessly. It took only a split second to imagine the scene. Mattie, sitting contentedly on the ground, rooster carcass between her front legs while she studied the problem, white meat or dark?

"Oh no, Michele. That's terrible. Do we know whose rooster it is?" (Maybe I can pick up a replacement rooster on the way home. Where do they sell roosters, anyway?)

"No. I called Buddy and asked if he knew of anyone missing a rooster, and he said it sounded like we were having chicken stew tonight."

"Bless you, Buddy."

"Uh oh. The rooster's up again."

"You mean it's still ALIVE?"

"Of course. Mattie's been carrying it around by its neck. It's her new toy."

"This is a joke, right?"

"Hardly."

"Well, can't you get her to just let it loose?"

"No, that's why I'm calling you. She loves her new rooster. He's lost a lot of feathers on his neck, though."

"Call Sherry Rind. She'll know what to do. She's a chicken person."

"Who's Sherry Rind?"

"Never mind."

So help me, I had this conversation this week. And the rooster's still around, staying in the woods somewhere close by. And Mattie likes to get him and bring him home to play. A neighbor called Michele on Friday, and asked her to call Mattie, "She's down here with a rooster in her mouth." I know Mattie is taken with this rooster. I wonder what the rooster thinks about his new best friend?

* * *

All this talk of Airedale sleep habits has reminded me of Murphy, my most previous Airedale. Murphy left us last January, just after his first birthday. I guess we'll never know where he went, but my suspicion is that he was dognapped, possibly by one of the workmen who built the house next door. And why not? He probably had the best temperament of any Airedale, or any dog I've ever known. He left a hole in our hearts that may never fill. There just won't be another Murphy.

Murphy had his own bed, and sometimes Michele would bring out an old quilt for him to snooze on in the front hall. He didn't pass up many opportunities to nap during the day. At night, though, it was different. Murphy always slept directly on the floor, right beside me. Sometimes I would hang my arm over the side in the middle of the night, just to touch him, and his presence would be strangely reassuring. Similarly, he would sometimes nose me in the middle of the night, just to make sure I was there, and I hope my presence re-assured him, as well.

I remember a morning a year or so ago. It was still dark out, and while I was still more asleep than awake, I became aware of my wife snuggled close against my backside. "Mmmmm," as I inched back-ward, trying to tighten the spoons, and take in even more of her warmth. As I lay there with my beloved, it seemed like perfect tran-quility, perfect peace. This must be the better part of "for better or worse." No, it was the best. As the sleep dissolved, I was overcome with an urge to kiss Michele, not deeply or passionately-I didn't even want to wake her. I just wanted to give her a tiny, tender kiss. Very slowly I turned toward her and offered perhaps the slightest, but most heartfelt kiss ever.....but Michele, you're so hairy. Michele, you smell! MURPHY! Get OFF the bed! OFF MURPHY! NOW! Oh, good morning, Michele. Didn't mean to wake you.

* * *

OK, OK, we've all had our fun picking on the unthinking, un-feeling, unloving, self-centered, dog-hating husbands of the world. May I have just a moment to comment on the recent OUTRA-GEOUS behavior of my wife? I really didn't think she would do this. I didn't even think she was capable of it. Not after 22 years of marriage, 2 wonderful daughters, and 2 Airedales, a Dachshund, a Lab, a Boxer, an Australian Shepherd, and a pound dog - but she did. I just can't imagine what has gotten into her. Up to now Michele has been a perfect wife - in every way. But something has turned, her dark side is suddenly coming to the surface, and I am at a loss to ex-plain it.

Do you know what she did Friday afternoon? Right after I got home and greeted all the dogs, and then her? I've been depressed all weekend, it's so insensitive. She had the audacity to declare, in no uncertain terms, and right in front of not only our children (it had been a bad day already for their tender ears) but also Mattie, Roscoe, and Doc, that they were no longer human - that from now on they were JUST DOGS. Like a crazy woman she shouted that they had better get used to being outside, because that's where they were staying. She was upset about the dirt in our bed and the sofa, and the floor, and about the fleas that turn up sometimes unexpectedly, and about being awakened in the middle of the night 2 or 3 times, and about the blue cheese Mattie had just eaten, and I guess there were a few other things. Gee. I thought we'd worked through all that. What to do?

* * *

Oh, no. I was afraid this day would come - when the topic of temperament and trustworthiness came up. Yes, there are people out there who think Airedales cannot be trusted. While I disagree with this notion, I must, begrudgingly, acknowledge that a few people out there might have reason to feel this way. Is there any room on this list for negative observations about our Airedales? About when they're not so cute?

I've owned five Airedales over the years, and without a doubt, the most famous, the best remembered, the most infamous, the most notorious of them all was Josh, at least within a small circle of friends. I've reported some of his funnier antics to this list, but I've kept to myself some of his minor (and major) transgressions. Someday I'll write down the story of how the Town of Lookout Mountain, Tennessee got a leash law. Yes, Josh was right there -he was the father of the law, one that is detested by the citizenry to this day. But I digress....Josh came to me as a puppy, and he was always, from day one, a mixture of good and bad (aren't we all?). Like many, I tended to emphasize the good, and overlook the bad. While I saw, for the most part, a goofy Airehead, others, to be frank, saw a big, powerful, fearsome beast who, to be on the safe side, ought to be feared.

In those days people didn't get upset about dogfights the way they do now, and Josh certainly was involved in his fair share, and I dare say he whupped many a butt in his time. In my youth, I thought this was cool, and my adolescent ego rather enjoyed having the toughest dog around. But even so, there comes a point....

Back to Sky Valley Pioneer Camp. We kept 3 pigs every summer, and would slop them with the leftovers three times a day. By the end of the summer, they'd be fattened up, and on their way to market. Every summer, at least once, the pigs would escape the pen, and for a few days, until they could be captured, would take their slop from outside the pen, rather than inside. Have you ever tried to catch a pig? Probably not, since they outlawed greasy pig chases. Rest assured, it's damn difficult. They're quick. If you haven't already guessed, Josh got into a little trouble when the pigs got out. I heard the most awfulest racket off in the woods, and a few moments later, here comes Josh, blood all over his face, and the camp had one less pig.

So help me, that one incident changed Josh forever. Maybe it was the taste of blood, I don't know, but he was not the same afterward. Yes, he was the same around people, same old goofball, but around four legged ones, he was always a danger. I saw him go after a horse once, went for the neck. The horse had the sense to turn and kick him. He caught Josh square on the jaw, and he went flying. I thought Josh might be dead, but he just got up and went back for more.

It gets worse. Later that same summer, while hiking in the Pisgah Forest, we had stopped for lunch. From the mountain side behind us, all of a sudden down came a fawn deer, running for its life and making a noise I had never heard before, Josh on its heels. I was able to catch Josh before he actually attacked, but the deer, literally fell over dead, I think from fright alone.

Josh stayed with me for another 2 years, one year living in inner-city Memphis. He and I had a wonderful bond between us, but I hate to say he was one Airedale who could not be trusted. Temperament? Boy, did he ever have one. Come to think of it, why on earth did I ever get another Airedale? I guess because, as we all know and understand, they are not all like that, and thankfully, the good heart of an Airedale can outweigh all others.

* * *

There's a thread running on the AOL Airedale board about the wonderful and sometimes magical habit of our beloved Airedales' opening, or just passing through, closed doors. It has brought to mind an old story. A few of you may remember Josh, the Airedale of my twenties, the one who accompanied me to summer camp, and bit me so impolitely on the way to Morning Dip. (Ed. note: published in Houses Full of Laughter.) What a dog he was. The good, the bad, the ugly - all those things. Seems like Josh was forever getting either the credit or the blame for just about everything that happened around me, and it was usually deserved.

This is another of Josh's adventures at Sky Valley Pioneer Camp, a tiny boys camp tucked away deep in the mountains of western North Carolina. During this summer I served as the counselor of the 15 year olds, the counselors-in-training, and we lived separate and apart from the rest of the camp, across the lake. For the most part, we had our own program and did our own thing. Josh, of course, was the mascot of the Trail Blazers, as we were called, and he went with us everywhere. On this particular Sunday, I came up with the idea that we would forego the usual Sunday chapel service at camp and go, instead, to Sunday services at the Blue Ridge Baptist Church, a landmark that we had walked by countless times in our travels throughout the vicinity. Seemed like a good idea at the time, so I had the boys put on their cleanest T-shirts and off we went on the 5 mile trek down the Cedar Mountain Road to the Blue Ridge Baptist Church, Josh staying with us every step of the way.

Now you need to understand that this church is located about five miles from the nearest paved road, and the church itself is just a small, one-room structure, neatly kept, but nothing fancy. I suppose there were about 30 people there when the 8 of us arrived. As we entered the church, I admonished Josh to stay outside as I pulled the door shut behind me. Once in my pew, I could see Josh through the open windows running around the church, looking for an entry, first this way, then that, to no avail. The place was secure. After a time, he settled down, and I could see him amusing himself in the side yard-you know, just doing Airedale things. Soon it was time for a hymn, and the congregation let loose with "When the Roll Is Called Up Yonder." And I mean let loose-the building shook. Josh, hearing this, came running and stood up on the window sill with that happy Airedale look. Then he pointed his nose skyward and let loose with a howl of his own, the one he had previously reserved only for passing sirens. AWOOOOOOOOOLLLLL. The congregation didn't stop, and neither did Josh, and I thought I would die. Down Josh! Quiet Josh! Finally the hymn was over, and I may as well have been under the pew. I was the only one who wasn't laughing.

We all managed to compose ourselves, and the service continued, Josh back to doing whatever it was he was doing. Best I remember, the preacher gave a rousing sermon, and toward the end he offered a rather lengthy prayer on a wide range of topics, many of them touching the concerns of the church family. The prayer was heartfelt, and all had their heads bowed reverently, many with eyes closed. As the prayer continued, I heard the preacher, "And please, dear Lord, deliver us from the big ole R-dale a'coming down the aisle rite now." Amen.

Susan Olsen

Contributors and Rescue Contacts 🐾

Following is a list of Airedale Rescue contacts, according to region:

Barbara Curtiss (New England) 860-927-3420;sculpturedale@hotmail.com
Joey Fineran (PA/NJ/DE) 610-294-8028
Candy Kramlich (NY) 914-428-0017
Lou Swafford (Mid-Atlantic) 301-572-7116; swafford@erols.com
Linda Baake(South Central) 252-637-3575; lynaire@aol.com
Donna Noland (Gulf States) 205-823-6666; Djsdosido@aol.com
Sally Schnellmann (Florida) 561-219-2222; Airemann@aol.com
Carol Domeracki (Midwest) 231-276-6390; atratc@aol.com
Becky Preston (Texas) 817-485-7041; skycladd@flash.net
Connie Turner (Northwest) 503-399-9819; CTurner859@aol.com
Sandy Pesota (California) 805-245-1257; blkjack@frazmtn.com
Melissa Moore (Southwest) 602-996-9648; chapelec@earthlink.net
Carol Dickinson (Alaska) 907-345-2787; ddced@alaska.net

William W. Austin, Bill, lives in the greater Atlanta, GA, area with his wife (Cathy), son (Nicholas) and two ADT's Merlin and Sarah. He reports: I was originally a physicist, then sang opera for a living for several years. These days I am a computer geek for a living. Merlin's real name is Sam's Dandy Merlin-Dale; he has shown in both agility and obedience. Sarah is Sarah Endipitty Dale, the true ADT from Hell.

Bilbo and Frodo the HobbitDales, better known as "twin dogs" to the neighborhood kids, reside in the Shire of Ann Arbor, Michigan with their uprights Skip and Becky Barcy, and two Marmelade Tabby Cats (Pixel and Puck).

Karl Broom is a Senior Analyst with Science Applications International Corporation. He and his wife, Joyce, live in Great Falls, Virginia where their lives are owned and operated by Airedales Geoffrey and Brady. Earlier this year, Karl passed up a golden opportunity to remain silent and he is now the distributor for To Aire is Divine.

Judie Burcham, Brian, Maggie Airedale, Zebulon Pike (alpha male cat) and Trixie ("I am the only alpha cat and I am female") live in Chesapeake, Virginia. Maggie is their first Rescue Airedale but not their first Airedale. For Brian, Airedales have become the way of the world.

'Dale Burrier lives in Ohio and is active with his 3 ADTs in Hunting & Working training and events.

At home, in Sharon Massachusetts, Debbie (Kiwi) Carley works as a self-employed Public Relations professional and is a studying for her MA in Communications Management. In 1999, she introduced her personal line of hand-crafted Airedale tiles via the internet. Kugel, Debbie's ADT serves as her web mascot. Please visit their web site at: http://www.starfishdesign.com/traditions.

Randall & Sandra Cooley's kennel is Strongbow Airedales, family dogs for show and field, located at 1606 16th Avenue; Grafton, WI 53024; (414) 377-7852, RLCDALES@aol.com. They are the proud owners of Ch. Moraine Prime Minister, JHV, SHV, the first champion ADT to earn a Senior Hunter Versatile title!

Denise Cuevas lives in Nanuet, New York, a suburb of New York City, with father Frank and fiancee Larry. She's dog mom to Airedale Terrier Max aka Maxie Doodle, Lab/Pointer Mix Shadow aka Me and My Shadow, C*t Sheena aka the Weener and C*t Harley aka Harley Barley or Harley Bob Marley. Denise is a Business Consultant currently with Metropolitan Life Insurance.

Jeanine Dara lives in Belgium with Airedale Red. She designed and donated the web site for the first listbook, Houses Full of Laughter.

Jadie Davis lives in an Illinois wooded cul-de-sac protected by "ADT Security" Zak (8yo) and puppy Rhuster (Royalcrest's Rhuah Rigel). The pack is herded by Tassie the OES lassie. Their website is http://www.geocities.com/Heartland/1364/friendsdavispack3.html.

Dorothy Dunn Duff drives between plots in Dallas and Tijeras, New Mexico chaperoned by Airedale Miss Madie (aka Rescue Darling of the Southwest) and Oscar (aka Little Napoleon) and occasionally her husband, Will. In her free time (when she is not picking up poop, feeding crows or planting the next crop) she wears a psychologist's hat.

Active ATRA volunteers Patty Eisenbraun and her husband Ken live in Michigan with their three Airedales, Ivy (rescue), Annie (rescue) and Poppy, aka the 'Silly Sisters'. Patty is a freelance artist who does handcrafted and painted pieces featuring Airedales, including chairs, mailboxes, small paintings, antiques tin boxes and other 'found' items. A donation from the sale of each item is given to ATRA. Her web site, Airedale-Arts.com is in the works. For more information on some very unique Airedalia, contact her at airecare@aol.com.

Mary Gade, the intrepid hero of Piper's story, heads up Midwest Rescue. She spends much of her "spare" time as a pooper scooper living in Cedar Rapids, with her husband Milt and Airedales Dolly & Clancy, who are busy "guardin the yard" in their rural Iowa home.

Mary Giese lives in Lawrence, Kansas with Charlie, Nell and Toggle. They can be seen at www.geocities.com/Heartland/1364/paradegiese.html (courtesy of Andrea Denninger). Mary practices law and handles rescue for ATCA in Kansas and western Missouri.

Christie and Denys Hansen live in Springfield, MO with ADT Katie, the three year old, spoiled rotten pup.

Joanne Helm, Indus Kennels, Calgary, Alberta, I have raised Airedales in the Calgary area for 20 years. Indus Kennels, 403-236-9296, is home to Int. &Can. Ch Terydale HK King of Indus, breeding fine quality puppies of excellent temperment. Web site: http://www.cadvision.com/helmj. Airedale Pet Grooming Video: Learn how to make your dog look great is at http://www.cadvision.com/helmj/groomvid.html.

Michael Jones and his wife Judith Powers are held hostage in St. Petersburg, Florida by Chester, his sister Hanna and Willie recently freed from a pet store cage. Michael is a woodworker doing custom work on yachts (and agility equipment), Judith is an artist and director of the Pinellas County Arts Council.

Dan Joyce is a software support person & Tania is a nurse who works in a rehabilitation hospital. We live in Melbourne, Australia with our two Airedale terriers, Reba (Oldiron With Attitude) and Gillian (Oldiron X-Files Gillian), and Harpo our 11 year old Aussie terrier X.

Randy and D'Arlene-Anne Kapenga live in Michigan where Randy works for Public Broadcasting and I am involved with a Miss Dig notification service..Our first ADT was and is Misty, now 12, who has outlived her pups Rosie and Ben, who lived with us. Now we have My Heart's Rainbeau, called Beau, our rescue 'Dale.

My name is Marc Lawrence and I live in Sydney, Australia with Peter, Monty(Airedale) and Homer (the c*t). My job is computer stuff. Monty's posh name is Strongfort Spreadeagle, out of US dog, Serendipity's Eagle's Wings and Aussie bitch Strongfort Solaris. Monty's title is "Just a Pet," and I'm pretty happy with that. Check out http://www.ozemail.com.au/~marclaw/monty.htm.

Mary Lukaszewski, Norwalk, CT, has been showing and breeding Airedales in obedience and conformation since 1986. She is also an obedience instructor. She bred and showed Standard Schnauzers for over 20 years prior to breeding Airedales.

Barbara Mann is a statistics professor in Ohio who is tolerated because she buys the dog food by Barney and Gus, or, more formally: U-CDX Seneca Barnaby Butterbur, CDX, CGC and Seneca Gambler's Gusto, CD. She also teaches obedience classes for the Dayton Dog Training Club.

Jack McLaughlin is a breeder exhibitor since 1971 with 11 finished champions from his breeding, the Altena Pack. He and his wife, Doris, live in a moderate sized doghouse in Hockessin, DE. They are retired from industry but continue to manufacture and sell Macknyfe strippers, Deetailers, and Muckrakers. See the website at: http://members.aol.com/macknyfe/ for descriptions, prices and ordering instructions for these fine tools.

Judy McLaughlin lives in Somerville, Massachusetts. Judy spent 20-odd years as an ADT sibling. With so much resultant subject matter in her background, she naturally turned to writing as a career. She is Jack and Doris' daughter.

Mary Melton is a telecommuting technical editor living with her family in Everett, WA. Libby the ADT brings joy and mischief to the Melton house.

Yvonne M. Michalak, R.N. works at The Childrens Hospital of Buffalo, New York. She is an assistant trainer in agility for the Hamburg All Breed Obedience (Dog) Club. Branagan , Georgia, and I train almost every day in Obedience, Agility and Tracking. Both Airedales received their CGC titles last summer and became Canine Good Citizens.

Ronna Miller, a retired pediatric surgeon, lives with her husband, Brian Cornelius, an architect/designer, in "Dale-as," Texas. They are the houseguests of ADT Moxie (Stirling's Whiterock Moonbeam), who is planning a career in Agility with titles to be dedicated to her dearly departed and much loved predecessor, Gracie, Princess of Punk.

Peter Mortensen lives with his wife Charlotte in Denmark. Peter is a refrigeration engineer and Charlotte is a registered nurse. They are owned by Sophie (Spicaway Talk of the Town) and Tenna (Spicaway Well-Turned). Their homepage is located at www.airedale.dk.

Kirk Nims is a Librarian/Webmaster in Birmingham, MI who owns, along with Michael Billion, a Prototype Vehicle Technician, rescue'dales Miles (Sir Miles' Doo Bop) and Andy IV.

Donna Noland lives on Dosido Farm outside Birmingham, Alabama with her husband John, two phantom cats, and three Airedales: DJ's Highland Walker (Walker), DJ's Highland Dosido Girl (Dosi), and Cripple Creek Copacabana (Lola. Walker is John's "boat-riding, beer-drinking buddy". Dosi does therapy work through the Delta Society and has her CGC. Lola has crowned herself Queen.

Kanako Ohara is a graduate student in sociolinguistics at Georgetown University, Washington, DC. She and her Airedale Tekoah Teddy Bear Necessity currently reside in NYC.

Susan Olsen lives in Franklin, North Carolina in the Smoky Mountains. I am an artist who does a rare technique of paper making, "The Paper is a Painting." My rescue Kuta passed away last year, and a new little Airedale princess, Chaka Pawnee, has come into my life, daughter of Indus' Kennel's prized Drew,"King of Indus."

Margarita Revzin, I live with my husband and son in North Potomac, Maryland. We came to the USA from Russia 10 years ago. Both my husband and I are programmers and enjoy it. Max is our first dog and we hope to compete in obedience.

Sherry Rind is a poet and freelance writer living with her family in Redmond, WA. Editor of this and the previous book, Houses Full of Laughter, she keeps her blood pressure low by working out with Darwin (Ironcroft Aria QED) and Keeper (Highland Keepn' In Trouble).

Michelle Rolandson's ADT is Whitecliff Wind n th' Willows, a/k/a Willow, the Master Huntress of Fire Flies. Michelle is a Bank Manager - Independent Bank South Michigan-residing in Mason, Michigan, "but the whole world is our home!"

Shirley Sanborn lives with ADTs Otis and Milo Sanborn in Laconia, New Hampshire. Both boys have a job, going to work with mom as a courier. Otis sits in the front and watches the road. Milo sits in the back and watches the boxes. (Otis saw early fame as the cover model for Houses Full of Laughter and never lets his brother Milo forget it.)

Barbara Schneider lives in Virginia Beach, VA and has bred Airedales since 1984. Serendipity Airedales is the home of the top Best in Show winning Airedale in the history of the breed, Ch. Serendipity's Eagle's Wings, otherwise known as Peter. With limited breeding, he was also the #1 Airedale sire for 1997 and the #2 sire for 1998. His sister, Serendipity Rejoices (Joy), was the #1 Airedale dam for 1998. Our dogs have frequently been included in the "top ten" breed listings. Write to SerendipityAiredales@worldnet.att.net or visit http://members.tripod.com/~SerendipityAiredales/.

Steen Selvejer is a TV-producer/reporter living near Odense in Denmark with his wife, two children and ADTs Spicaway Lonely Rider (Nakki) and Spicaway Zorba. They participate in conformation, agility, and are about to take up tracking. Web site: http://www.geocities.com/Heartland/Pointe/ 2900.

Chuck Shaddoway claims to be a lowlife desert rat from northern Nevada, and has delusions about being a writer. Mr. Woofer has no need for titles; his reputation carries enough weight.

After working full-time at the Texas Dept of Health as a Medicaid program administrator, Cheryl Silver returns home in Austin to begin the second shift as maid, chauffer, door opener, cook, etc., to her gang of seven furkids, six of whom are rescues. Henry my Honey, my delightfully devilish Daisy, and Hurricane Gracie form the Airedale contingent.

Pip Smith is an Airedale fancier and breeder who lives in North Vancouver, BC Canada with her two Airedales - Trubble (Cuvaison's Ms. Demeanor) and Wiley (Ironcroft Live Wire Phaireborn) - and sometimes her Mom Margaret's Airedale Darley (Cdn. Ch. Phaireborn Spirit of the Cove). She is a computer consultant and is deeply involved with several purebred dog clubs. Pip is the Chief Evaluator for BC for the St. John Ambulance Therapy Dog Program where Trubble is an active member and Wiley is a Therapy Dog-in-training.

Cover designer Roberta Sparr lives in Missoula, MT, with her two ADTs Thelma (7) and Charlie (1), and three cats. She has a MFA in painting and drawing and works in a family business. Her works have been shown in "100 Years of Women's Art" in Montana; regional exhibits in MT, Wyoming, Washington, and Oregon; and some national exhibits. Her painting "Annie" won first place in the professional category at the Spokane Canine Art Exhibit. The model for the cover art illustration is Charlie (Morning Star's Charlie Bear) and the medium is graphite on Bateman Cover Series.

Abbe Stashower lives in Seattle, WA with her husband, Saul, a merchant marine, and son Jacob. Sequoyah's Talkalot; aka; Sadie is 10 years old and CH. Ten Acre Wood's Tigger; aka; Tigger is Sadie's son and 7 years old.

Kari Stielow and her family Craig, Jake-nonfur (5), Jenna-nonfur (1) and Zoe, the 6 mth. old furbaby, live in White Bear Lake, Minnesota. Zoe's registered name is "Rainbow's Morning Frost."

Dave Weaver is a civil engineer living in Morrison, Colorado with his two sparedales: the lovely and spirited Abigale Agatha Airedale and the rowdy, impetuous, and handsome, Rusty Airedale.

Gena Welch, the founder and 'ListMom' for Airedale-L, teaches middle-school children at the Chattanooga School for the Creative Arts, and moon-lights as a water aerobics instructor at the local YMCA. Gena and her husband, John Fernandez, live with: The Lovely Rita, the inspiration for Airedale-L, Ellie 'JB' McFearsome, the perrenial 70 lb. puppy, and Photon, the Colonel and Poster Child for Elderly Dog Rescue.

Terry Wertan and her husband Lawrence live in Lavonia, GA with Duke and Katie Mae. Their publishing house, Boxer Books, currently offers Lawrence's Airedale books The Lost Champion and International Grand Crown, as well as the 1921 reprint of The Airedale for Work and Show by A.F. Hochwalt. Their web site is www.alltel.net/~wertan.

Christie Williams (West Lafayette, Indiana) is a professor at Purdue University, specializing in Plant Genetics. She is being trained for agility by her two young Airedales. Erin, a beguiling Rescue, and Argus. Her web pages are: http://www.vsm.cape.com/~bailey/dogs/erin.html and http://www.vsm.cape .com/~bailey/dogs/rigel.html.

RickWilliams, a meterologist, lives in Victoria, British Columbia, with his wife Doris and three year old Brandy, who has the distinction of having 13 siblings. She's been to obedience classes and played the role of the class clown V-E-R-Y well

Kent Young writes: I am a chimney sweep and window cleaner in Northern Colorado. Cosmo A Dale is a rescue from the ADTRL in Broomfield. He arrived looking like anything but an ADT but when cleaned and clipped, he looked classic. It took more than a year to socialize him to other dogs and people.